# The Bloodline
## A Draegonstorm Novel

NOVELS IN THE DRAEGONSTORM: ELDERS SAGA

# The Bloodline
## A Draegonstorm Novel
### K.R. Fraser

Dragonrock
Press

DRAGONROCK PRESS

THE BLOODLINE
PREQUEL TO DRAEGONSTORM: BLOOD FEUD

Published by Dragonrock Press, a division of Dragonrock Enterprises Inc.
Copyright © 2021 by K.R. Fraser
Foreword copyright © by K.R. Fraser

Dragonrock Press, Dragonrock, and the Dragonrock logo are all
trademarks of the Dragonrock Enterprises Inc. group of companies.
Dragonrock ® is a registered trademark of Dragonrock Enterprises Inc.

Cover art by Leon Cross Designs

A Dragonrock Book
Published by Dragonrock Press, LLC
Langhorne, PA. 19047

This is a work of fiction. All of the characters, organizations and events
portrayed in this novel are either products of the author's imagination or
are used fictitiously, and any resemblance to actual persons, living or dead,
business establishments, events, or locations is completely coincidental.

ISBN 978-1-7333787-9-6
Printed in the United States of America

*For Chere, who believed in me before anyone else did,*
*and for the many wonderful conversations about our favorite world over*
*lunch.*
*For Beth, for loving me as only a sister could.*
*You have been the most wonderful and supportive friend I could ever ask*
*for.*
*For Scorpi, for always being a friend, even when her own life is in turmoil.*
*For Kimmi, for being the amazing fan I never even knew she was.*
*For Stacey, for loving me unconditionally through some really rough*
*times, and never walking away.*
*For Tracy, who was my friend through some of the toughest years of both*
*our lives.*
*I miss our walks and our many talks. You were taken from us way too*
*soon.*
*I love you, lady, and I miss you so much.*
*For my lost children, no matter where you are or what you are doing,*
*you are still loved, cherished and carried with the hope in my heart*
*that you will one day find your way back home.*
*For my friend, John, who calls me every Friday for my Minecraft fix.*
*For Tony, who has put up with so much from me in spite of everything.*
*And most importantly, for Jim, for keeping me on schedule, never letting*
*me quit, checking in on me,*
*and just keeping me going through one of the hardest years of my life.*
*Words alone can never express my love and gratitude*
*to one of the most amazing people I have ever known.*
*You have helped me to grow stronger and better, and to find the Dragon*
*buried in me again.*
*No one could ever be closer than you are to me.*

*~ Te Iubesc ~*

DEDICATED TO TRACY MCDONALD
YOU WILL ALWAYS BE LOVED, CHERISED AND RESPECTED.
WE MISS YOU.
02/01/1964 – 02/16/2021

# Table of Contents

## Foreword

The world of Draegonstorm has been an exciting journey for a great many people since its inception, and it has been a thrilling ride every step of the way for me personally. I never imagined that what began as stories for my children would grow to become such an incredible adventure. Yet, here we are. There were so many roadblocks getting to this point that had to be overcome. However, quitting has never been my style, and my closest friends would not let me give up. So I kept at it and fought my way through everything that stood in the way of my success. I wanted to be sure this story would see its way into the hands of those who wanted to journey into the magical realm of the impossible. My hope is that within these pages, each of you will discover a journey to another world, and that you will find those Unicorns and Dragons I see behind every waterfall or tree. I hope when you discover the magic of my world, you will fall in love with every remarkable moment I did when I created it.

I cannot encourage you enough to try and stick to what you love. Dare not only to dream about it, but to pursue it until it becomes a reality. There was a time when I believed this to be an impossible dream. There were even members of my own family who ridiculed me for its pursuit. Even among those who did support me, some hoped for my success, but thought it would never truly become a reality.

Sometimes just knowing others want you to succeed is enough to give you the drive to keep moving steadily forward, and with every step closer to achieving my goal, those closest to me began to realize it was going to happen and started cheering me on with every breath. There is no word in existence that can describe the feeling that passes through you when you finally reach such a difficult goal. It is a turning point in your life that sets you on a whole new path in your journey. I have fallen in love with every step this journey has taken me on, and I hope when you read the stories and travel with these characters through their many adventures that you will love reading about them as much as I loved creating them.

Happy reading!

K.R. Fraser

# The Bloodline
## A Draegonstorm Novel

## Chapter One
## Mastric's Law

*When I looked back and saw just how deep the truth ran, I realized we were chosen solely for what we possess. We were his before we ever even knew of his existence.*
*~ Reivn ~*

The underground waterway was pitch black, cold and damp... its wet, algae-covered walls silent save for the gentle lapping of water against the side of a single dock that led to a door above. Unknown to man, the lake had existed for countless centuries, and was commanded by an ancient and powerful entity that even the Immortals feared. Rarely ventured into, it remained undisturbed... until now.

Elena opened the door and hurried down the steps, followed by two servants bearing torches to light the way. Her soft blonde hair caught the light, giving her an almost ethereal appearance as she scanned the vast dark cavern. A gentle breeze drifted across the water, rippling her pale blue gown and she shifted nervously, smoothing it down before continuing her vigil. Finally, the light splashing of water against the bow of a boat caught her attention. Motioning for one of her escorts to hold his torch higher, she tried to see through the thick black mist that blanketed the entire tunnel, but she was no match for his magic. She would not see him until he wanted her to. Her delicate, porcelain-like face contorted with worry until she spotted the dinghy coming up the channel toward her.

A cloaked and hooded passenger stood alone in the center of the boat. When it finally came to a stop alongside the dock, a rope rose into the air and secured itself to a piling. The small craft stilled, and he levitated up and onto the decrepit platform leading up to the landing.

"Wait here," Elena told her escorts. She hurried down to greet him and curtsied low before kissing his hand. "Prosperitas vobis, Abbas. Welcome back, my lord," she stated apprehensively, hesitating a second before adding, "I heard the rumor. Is it true?"

Mastric nodded. The master of magic was a daunting sight and bred fear in those around him. Dressed in a black cowled robe, only the deep blue magic emanating from his eyes and the glyph on his forehead were visible beneath its hood. He was not amused at having been summoned back from his seclusion so soon. He had planned on spending far more time in the pool's depths to commune with its ancient knowledge. "It is," he replied, his irritation very apparent. "Gather the others at once."

"Yes, father." Elena kissed his hand again and stepped aside.

Mastric floated past her in silence. But he stopped unexpectedly at the bottom of the stairs, held out his hand, and motioned for her to join him.

She hurried over and together they climbed the ancient stone staircase that led to the Guild above.

The servants watched as the mooring line detached itself from the piling, dropping back down into the boat before it eerily glided out across the water to disappear once more into the mist... as silently as it had first appeared. Once it was out of sight, they headed up the steps, leaving the underground lake once more in darkness.

Mastric drifted down the corridor in silence.

Elena knew he would not discuss what had happened until they were all assembled, so she focused on the telepathies to her brethren. However, when she sent out the summons, she felt a twinge of guilt, remembering the last punishment one of them had suffered and wondered if this would be another such outcome.

The Elders had gathered by the time Mastric and Elena reached the Great Hall and the room was buzzing with conversation. It silenced the moment Mastric appeared.

He ignored them and glided over to his throne, only giving them his attention once he was settled. A cold chill moved through the room as he gazed at each of them in turn, making them more than a little uneasy. They all knew his temperament, and this latest news did not bode well.

Elena sat down next to him cautiously and waited for him to begin. Then she glanced at an empty seat, wondering again what would happen.

Seated across from her, her brother Valfort followed her gaze, rubbing the scruff on his chin and smiling at her naivety. Then pushing his dark hair out of his eyes, he leaned back and crossed his arms to wait. He had heard the rumor too, but he believed it greatly exaggerated. *Surely father would never tolerate such a blatant disregard for the rules. Even Reivn is not so favored that he would ignore it. If the rumor is true, his victory will not help him... not after his last failure. If there is even a little truth to it, then he has gained father's wrath.* He snickered at the thought.

Mastric instantly turned on him. "Something amuses you, Ceros?" The threat in his voice was unmistakable.

Valfort's smile instantly disappeared, and he shook his head. "No, my lord," he answered humbly, righting himself in his chair. He fell silent and lowered his eyes. He had no desire to garner his father's attention. He knew all too well what Mastric's notice entailed. Memories of recent nights hanging on his laboratory wall were still too fresh in his mind for comfort, and he rubbed his skin, still feeling the pain he had endured for months.

Long minutes passed in absolute silence until the elders wondered what they were waiting for. Finally, Elena drew a slow deep breath and looked up to meet Mastric's gaze. "My lord, has he been summoned, or are we going to discuss this without him?" She shook inwardly, knowing the brutal temper he had, but as his mate, she also knew he would not truly harm her, regardless of his anger.

Mastric glanced down in annoyance and shook his head. "I have already summoned him. He will arrive shortly."

They did not have long to wait. The doors opened and Reivn strode in, still wearing full armor and bearing his helm under his arm. His long black hair was in disarray, and he was covered head to toe in mud and blood. "Prosperitas Vobis, Abbas. I apologize for both my appearance and the delay. We were still clearing the last of the wounded when your message arrived. I came the moment I received it."

"I see." Mastric sat back and leaned on his hand, waiting for his youngest son to take his seat.

Reivn quickly assumed his place, noting his brothers and sisters were also present. He had not expected a full assembly of the Mastric's elders.

Finally, Mastric sat forward, leveling his gaze on Reivn. "You are here to answer for your disobedience. Before you say anything, send for the child. I would meet him myself."

Stunned by the demand, Reivn realized his recent befriending and turning of the man he now called his son had been discovered. "Father, I beg you to let me explain. Seth was wounded. We had been fighting side by side for months. He would have died..."

"Silence!" Mastric bellowed, his voice echoing with potent magic. "I do not want your excuses! I would see the child... now!"

Reivn tried to reason with him. "Father, I was going to present him..."

Mastric rose from his throne in a cold rage and lifted his hand. Reivn was immediately launched across the room by an unseen force, where invisible chains ensnared him and pinned him to the cold stone wall. Then purple and black flames materialized and enshrouded him. "Insolent pup! Do you think for a moment I will not destroy you? If you failed in your last mission, it will indeed be your fate. You can remain where you are until your son arrives. Now... summon him!"

Unable to argue further, Reivn closed his eyes as the magic licked at his skin, causing excruciating pain. Struggling to clear his mind, he telepathied his son. *Seth... It is time... for you to meet our creator. Come to me. Our shared blood... will guide you.*

The fire spell was one of Mastric's more cruel inventions. It served to keep the unruly in line. Known as *The Flames of Wrath*, it inflicted agonizing pain as though the flesh were being melted from their bones, but it did no damage to its unlucky victims.

Mastric ignored his suffering and turned to glare at the rest of his children. "Remember who is master here." Then he summoned a servant from the hall. "Lunitar! Fetch the other one!"

A servant appeared from the corridor beyond and bowed. Then his eyes wandered briefly up to Reivn before disappearing again.

In spite of his agony, Reivn had not missed his expression. It was an apology. Seeing Lunitar again reminded him of better nights, and he closed his eyes, focusing on the past to try and shut out the pain.

Lunitar and Reivn had been blood servants under Mastric for more than a thousand years together and were close friends. However, when Mastric elevated Reivn to a higher status as one of his own children, they had been forbidden to associate further. Mastric's rules concerning his children mingling with servants were strict. He viewed it as beneath them. So they had long since been unable to talk.

It was not long before Lunitar returned carrying an unconscious young man in his arms.

When Reivn caught sight of just who he carried, his eyes widened in spite of the pain. He recognized the youth. He had abandoned him to his fate in the mortal world more than fifteen hundred years ago. He stared at him in shock. This was not what he expected at all, and his stomach twisted in fear. Struggling against his bonds, he shifted his gaze to Mastric. His father was well-known for his merciless tactics when it came to keeping his own in line. "Father..." he cried in horror. "I know not what you have planned, but please..."

Mastric drifted across the floor effortlessly and took the unconscious man from Lunitar, dismissing him with a nod. Then he carried his prize to the center of the room and dropped him on the floor.

The youth did not wake, even when he hit the hard stone.

Lunitar bowed and quickly disappeared. He was under no illusion as to what would probably happen, and he could not bear to witness any further ruthlessness toward his only friend.

Elena closed her eyes. She knew how cold Mastric was and feared this would be yet another slaughter as a lesson to his son.

Even Valfort averted his gaze uncomfortably. This kind of cruelty was all too familiar to him.

However, Mastric merely stared at the man and waited.

It became clear what he was waiting for when footsteps were heard coming up the corridor, announcing another arrival.

Mastric opened the door with a mere thought.

A young blond-haired soldier stood in its threshold, somewhat confused by the assembly of Elders. Then he spotted Reivn suspended on the wall and engulfed by flames, and he took a step back.

"Stay where you are!" Mastric bellowed. His voice echoed with the power of the Spirals.

Seth was instantly rooted to the floor as if one with it. He stared up in fear as the Ancient glided over to him.

Reaching out boney fingers to grasp his shoulder, Mastric was on him blindingly fast, sinking fangs into his throat to taste his blood.

Valfort grinned as he watched the spectacle. He felt certain this would be a bloodbath. *You see, Reivn,* he telepathied his brother. *You try to reach higher than you should, and he will slap you back down where you belong... in the mud.*

Reivn closed his eyes, believing Mastric would indeed end the son he had created, knowing he would feel every second of it as it happened. He could already feel Seth's fear.

Mastric withdrew from Seth with a grin none could see under the shadow of his hood. *It would seem his blood is finding its own. This is even better than I imagined. Still, if I allow him too much indulgence, they will see my favor and seek to discover the reasons behind it. So, he must pay for his insolence.* He turned to gaze at Reivn, the glow from his eyes and glyph eerie in the torchlight as it grew in strength. "It would seem you at least chose well, but it matters not. I am claiming this one as your punishment for your failure to seek my consent."

Seth stared up at Reivn in horror. "No! wait! I..." He did not finish his sentence.

Mastric invaded Seth's mind and forced him into sleep. Then he dropped him on the floor as only minutes before he had done with the other man.

Leaving Seth where he laid, Mastric floated back to his other captive. He levitated the unconscious youth up into his arms again. "Since you want a son so badly, I will give you one."

Reivn's eyes filled with horror when he realized Mastric's intent.

Mastric sank his fangs in and drank until his prey's skin greyed as death threatened to claim him. But the master of magic was not finished. He pulled a vial of blood from his pocket and removed the stopper with a thought alone. Then he poured it down his helpless victim's throat.

Reivn closed his eyes. He knew whose blood was in that vial. He could already feel it, and he was screaming inside.

The young man began convulsing as the curse did its work, his color slowly shifting back to a healthier shade.

With a satisfied nod, Mastric lowered him back down to the floor. "I give you your son... Gideon."

Fearing for Seth now, Reivn begged for his elder son's life. "Father please... let Seth live!" He greatly feared Mastric's intent and stared at Gideon, who still laid at Mastric's feet, unable to conceal his thoughts.

Searching Reivn's mind, Mastric gazed at him in irritation. "Still defiant I see. Well, no matter. Seth is no longer your concern. He is mine to do with as I please." As he spoke, black mist engulfed Seth's body.

Reivn immediately felt the severing of the connection he shared with his son, and he stared hopelessly at the shroud enveloping him. Then it vanished, taking him with it.

"Seth's continued existence is now dependent on your obedience, so you had best remember your place," Mastric reminded him coldly.

Reivn closed his eyes. He knew he could not defy his father further and expect to live. And now, Seth's life was also in peril. Defeated, he lowered his head in obedience. "I am your loyal servant, my lord," he whispered.

With a smile, Mastric levitated Reivn down from the wall and removed the flames that tortured him. "You see? I can be reasonable."

Reivn immediately dropped to his knees, leaned forward, and touched his forehead to the floor. "Please forgive me, father."

Mastric stared at him for a moment before turning to his other children. "You have all born witness to your brother's punishment. Remember this, as it not the first time I have had to discipline one of you. Now leave! Reivn, you stay!"

All eleven of Reivn's brethren had mutely watched his torment, not daring to speak for fear of incurring Mastric's wrath. Now, most teleported from the room to remove themselves before he changed his mind.

Elena cast one last glance at Reivn. She could feel his suffering. Then acutely aware of Mastric's gaze as it shifted to her, she teleported out, leaving them alone.

Valfort almost wished he could stay, and had it not been for Mastric's direct order to disappear, he would have. Still, he knew better than to argue and reluctantly sauntered from the room to find amusement elsewhere.

Reivn did not move from his prostrate position. Keenly aware of the situation he was now in, he waited for permission, but he turned his head and his eyes ventured to Gideon, and he stared in stunned silence at the face he had thought dead centuries ago.

"Get up," Mastric commanded once the room had cleared. "I am not finished with you. There is still the matter of your mission to discuss."

Raising his head, Reivn slowly got to his feet. "My lord?"

Mastric glared at him. "Henry is dead as I commanded, yes?"

Reivn bowed. "Yes, my lord... in the tower. And no one saw me, as you commanded."

"And the Prince of Wales?" Mastric waited expectantly for his answer.

"He died on the battlefield at the hands of one of our men. York was victorious. Edward is clear to ascend the throne as you ordered." Reivn lowered his gaze again as he waited.

Mastric stood silently contemplating the significance of such a victory. He was pleased at how easily he had manipulated the human political arena yet again. Now England would slowly shift toward peace and civil unrest would cease, leaving him free to resume his plans. "You have done well. In spite of your foolish actions involving Seth, you still managed to please me. So, I am inclined to grant you a reward. Name it."

"My son, Seth... at my side," Reivn replied, hope filling his eyes. "Please let him go, father."

His eyes narrowing, Mastric growled. "You test my patience. I told you... he is mine."

Then Reivn remembered someone else he had seen that night and he gazed at his creator boldly. "Then I ask for permission to have Lunitar... not just as my servant, but as my son."

Mastric stared at him in silence while he thought over the request. Finally, he chided, "Lunitar? He is nothing but a blood servant. I have already given you a son tonight. Why not pick something else? I could give you more power... make you stronger than Valfort has ever been. Would that not please you more than one more whelp to train?"

Reivn was adamant. He knew this might be his only chance to keep an old promise. "It matters not. I want him. You said to name my prize, and he is it. I swear I will not neglect Gideon's training. I will teach them both."

"A foolish request, but so be it. If you choose to squander this opportunity, I will not object." Mastric drifted to the door. "Take them both. Do not disappoint me again, or they will suffer for it."

Stunned that his request had actually been granted, Reivn stared at him for a second before coming to his senses. "Thank you, father!" he exclaimed, a smile crossing his features. Then he realized what he had been granted. "Lunitar!" he grinned, and closing his eyes, quickly sent out a telepathy to his friend. *Come to the great hall, and hurry.*

From his seat in the kitchen, Lunitar heard him and jumped up. Thinking Reivn must be in peril, he looked around to see if anyone was watching. Then he snatched a large knife from the counter and tucked it into his coat. He knew Reivn would never summon him unless it was serious. *This may not do any good, but they will at least know I was here... You do not stand alone, my friend.* Hurrying down the corridor, he played out scenarios in his head, trying to work out a way to help his friend. He knew his chances of actually doing so were slim, but he was determined to try. He briefly reached into his coat to reassure himself that the blade was still there. Then he entered the hall, keeping his eyes down.

"Lunitar! Good! You are here!" Reivn stated enthusiastically, his own relief causing him to momentarily forget how nervous Lunitar might be. "Come and help me with Gideon! We are going home!"

Completely taken by surprise, Lunitar glanced around, quickly realizing they were alone. Confusion crossed his features. "My lord?" he ventured cautiously, wondering if this was some test of Mastric's.

Seeing he was hesitant, Reivn grew serious. "You are free! Mastric has given you to me! You are finally coming to Draegonstorm, as I promised all those years ago! Before the night is out, you will be my son!"

## Chapter Two
## Freedom's Grace

Visibly shaken by Reivn's declaration, Lunitar paled slightly. He took a step back and stared at his friend in shock. Then when he realized Reivn was serious, he walked over and dropped the knife on a table. "Then I guess I won't be needing this," he stated, visibly relieved. "I won't ask how you managed this, but I am grateful."

Reivn gaped at him in total disbelief. "What could you possibly have done with that?" he asked.

"Whatever I could," Lunitar responded somewhat awkwardly. "I thought you were in trouble and needed my help. I swore to you long ago you would never stand alone. So, I had to try."

Gideon stirred at that moment, groaning as he grabbed his head . "aah, mihi enim ebrius nimis," he muttered, opening his eyes. Then he saw Reivn. "Quid? Quid tu hic?"

"English, you fool!" Reivn snapped.

Gideon sat up slowly. Disoriented, he struggled to clear the fog from his mind as he stared at his host in confusion. "Non intelligitis."

"Loqui anglicus," Lunitar stated.

Gideon looked downright baffled. "Quod anglicus?"

It dawned on Reivn that for whatever reason, Gideon did not know English. "He does not understand," he explained and knelt beside Gideon. Then before the young man could object, he put him back into a deep sleep, catching him as he fell over. Staring at him, Reivn contemplated some dark thought meant for him alone. Then he placed his hand on Gideon's forehead and entered his mind, traveling deep into his memories and thoughts back to birth. Leaving Gideon's knowledge of Latin and other languages intact, he added English to his dialects. As some memories passed, he clenched his jaw, forcing himself to ignore them. With brutal precision, he moved through each moment of Gideon's existence, and when he was finished, he deftly withdrew and woke him again. Then lying his son down again, he stood up and waited for him to come around.

Gideon finally opened his eyes and stared up at him groggily. "Quid... quid iustum accidit?"

Lunitar raised an eyebrow. "Anglicus."

Frowning as he struggled to sort the two languages out in his head, Gideon looked up. "Vos... uh... you... said you were not coming back."

Reivn's eyes grew dark and he was silent for a moment before answering. "I did not go back. My father did."

Sitting up slowly, Gideon looked around in confusion. "What are you... Wait. Where am I? The last thing I remember..." Then he frowned and scratched his head. "Actually, I do not remember much after that old man's visit."

"I did not see it in his mind. Nothing after..." Reivn was obviously agitated. He turned and stared in disgust at Gideon. "Where are they?"

"What?" Gideon got up, eyeing Reivn warily.

Reivn growled and took a step closer. "Your memories... where are they? I saw my father in your mind and then nothing! Answer me!"

Lunitar cleared his throat before politely interrupting. "Perhaps I can explain. He has been asleep for a long time... as far as I can tell, close to fifteen hundred years. I would wager to guess the old man he is referring to is Mastric and that visit would be when he first went to sleep."

Staring at the young man on the floor, Reivn growled in irritation. "Asleep for..." Then his eyes widened in realization. "Clever. He knew I wanted nothing to do with you and he brought you here as leverage. Now, I am saddled with a whelp I neither wanted nor created... willingly anyway. This is why the crafty bastard used my blood. He knew full well how I felt about you."

Gideon looked as though he had been struck. "I know what you think of me. You do not have to take care of me. I was doing so long before you met me. I can find my own way home." He was offended that Reivn thought he expected help, particularly considering their history.

His words hit a nerve. Reivn spun around and grabbed him by the throat, snatching him up from the floor. Then snarling in fury, he pulled him within inches of his face. "You have no idea what you are, do you? You are not human anymore and you certainly do not have the freedom to go where you will! Like it or not, I am now responsible for you!"

Just plain unnerved now, Gideon caught Reivn's hand and tried to pry himself free. "What in blazes are you talking about?" he choked out. "Let go of me! Why are you so angry?" He gasped for breath as Reivn's grip grew tighter. "I did not ask to be here! I understood how much you hated me last time we saw each other."

"Gideon," Lunitar quietly interjected. "You are making assumptions based on a life that no longer exists. This is the year 1472AD. The life you knew ended long ago. More than fifteen hundred years have passed since Mastric put you to sleep. In this world you are now part of, assumptions like yours will get you killed. Like it or not, Lord Reivn is now your master and father, as he will be mine."

Reivn dropped Gideon and turned away in frustration, not wanting to hear this himself. He knew what Mastric's so-called gift was intended for. It meant he would forever be face to face with the one person he had never wanted to see again. This was his true punishment.

Lunitar eyed Reivn's reaction with curiosity but decided it was best to leave any questions about their obvious history for another time. "You are now part of the Immortal world," he continued. "You are what the humans call a Vampyre... neither fully living nor dead. You can no longer eat food, nor walk in the sunlight. Blood is where you will draw your sustenance, and night is where you will live out your eternity. Ask for it or not, it is the reality you have been thrust into. It is neither gentle nor kind. And to be honest, having Reivn as our sire is one of the few mercies we will be shown from this night forward. Listen to him. Learn and grow, for if you do not, you will be destroyed." Then to set an example, he turned to Reivn and dropped to his left knee, crossing his right fist over his chest in salute. "My apologies for overstepping my bounds, my lord."

The night's events suddenly weighing heavily on him, Reivn walked over and pulled Lunitar to his feet. "You said what I could not. Now come. We have more to teach him, and your freedom has waited long enough."

Gideon looked from one to the other in shock. "You are both crazy! You seriously want me to believe this? Fifteen hundred years? That is impossible! What you even suggest is impossible! Father, if you wanted to punish me, there was no need to go to this charade!"

In the blink of an eye, Reivn grabbed him by the throat and bared his fangs, showing all the ferocity their kind was known for. "You have not earned the right to call me that! This is no joke, and I am even less amused than you! Now shut your mouth and do as you are told! Not another word, or I will end you!"

Paling considerably, Gideon gaped at Reivn, his eyes wide with fear as the sudden clarity of his situation sank in. He nodded comprehensively, too afraid to say any more.

Reivn put him down and turned to Lunitar. "Bring this fool. We are leaving. Do not worry about your belongings. We will send for them later." Then as an afterthought, he added, "...and please do not ask."

The full measure of his future filling his thoughts, Lunitar realized his life was about to change forever. "Yes, my lord," he replied, his voice filling with emotion. His loyalty was sealed with his freedom, and he would never look back. He walked over to Gideon and held out his hand. "Come... brother."

Without hesitation, Reivn opened a portal to his fortress home. Then he picked up his helm, nodded to Lunitar and stepped through.

Taking Gideon firmly by the arm, Lunitar followed Reivn without hesitation.

Gideon pulled back when he saw the swirling vortex in front of them. "By the Gods! What is that... thing?" he cried. His eyes filled with fear as he stared into the seemingly endless expanse of space.

"That is the door to your new home," Lunitar replied, trying not to smile. "Just close your eyes and I will guide you through."

Not at all ready to traverse what he viewed as foul magic, Gideon was shaking visibly when Lunitar pulled him into the portal. "Aah!" filled the empty room, as it snapped shut behind them. He was still screaming when they stepped out on the other side, but in seeing the grey stone walls, he blinked in surprise and stopped. "How did we... Is this real?" He was hesitant to voice his thoughts, but he had to know.

Lunitar shook his head in disbelief. "Did you really think it wasn't?" he chided. "Come."

Escorted by one of his guards, Reivn was waiting for them when they stepped down from the platform. "Welcome to Draegonstorm. This is your home from now on. Gideon, go with the guard, and he will get you settled. We will begin your education soon enough. However, I have business with Lunitar tonight you will not be privy to."

Not wanting to see his father's fury again, Gideon nodded silently and turned to leave. Then he paused and looked over his shoulder. "I know you are not pleased to see me, but I am not sorry to see you again. Perhaps now, I can make it right."

Reivn ignored him and turned to Lunitar. "Come with me."

His emotions a mix of relief and anxiety, Lunitar followed him in silence. He had waited for this for almost a thousand years, but now that it was here, he was nervous.

As they walked down the corridor, Reivn wondered where to begin. Finally he said, "If you are worried, do not be. It will be as painless as I can make it."

"I am not worried, my lord. I trust you. I will endure what I must, so I can finally fight at your side." Lunitar glanced at him, noting his silence.

In truth, Reivn was troubled, but he refused to voice what he was thinking. So he remained quiet as he led Lunitar the rest of the way to their destination.

When they reached the conservatory, they stopped. "The sun rises in an hour," Reivn stated. "I will have food and a bed brought here for you, as well as a servant who can see to anything you need throughout the day. Enjoy the sunrise. I will return for you at sunset."

Lunitar bowed, slightly humbled by his consideration. "As you command, my lord. I have one question, if I may."

"It is the eve of your rebirth, so ask what you wish," Reivn replied, wanting to make his transition as easy as possible. The memories of his own turning were still very dark, and his master had been brutal. He was not willing to subject Lunitar to that sort of suffering.

Looking around, Lunitar gazed in appreciation at the scenery. Then with a sigh, he asked, "Do you have a library?"

At his question, Reivn smiled. "I actually have quite a vast library."

"Then might I get a book to read?" Lunitar knew it was a strange request, but he wanted to begin his studies as soon as possible.

Taken aback by the question, Reivn raised an eyebrow. "You wish to do this on your last day in the sun?"

Lunitar was slightly embarrassed by his own boldness. "Honestly, my lord... my last day in the sun was over a thousand years ago. I have not been immersed as deep in the darkness as you all these years, but I have been living in its shadow. So I said my goodbyes to the light long ago."

Reivn stared at him in surprise. "Then you do not wish to wait until the morrow?" he asked quietly. He knew that to free Lunitar from the blood servant's bondage, there were only two options left after all these centuries... death or the turning. And he had committed himself to the latter the moment he had asked for Lunitar as his reward.

"My lord, I will do whatever you command, but I am ready now," Lunitar responded calmly. The more he thought about it, the more he wanted it done and behind him. Some small part of him still believed Mastric would come and reclaim him, just to punish Reivn further.

Silently mulling over how he wished to proceed, Reivn finally lifted his hand and covered Lunitar's eyes. Then summoning his birthright, he whispered, "Sleep. When you wake, you will be my son."

Lunitar collapsed, slipping into unconsciousness before he could respond.

Reivn caught him effortlessly. "I hope, old friend, that you will not later regret this," he whispered. Then he sank his fangs into Lunitar's throat and slowly drained him, careful not to damage the fragile life he held by a thread in his arms.

As he drank, Lunitar's blood sang to him, its chorus blending into his own at a molecular level and fusing at the genetic structure of the fluid itself. It was as though his own blood was greeting something it knew from another lifetime, and those echoes were giving birth to hazy images he did not understand. The similarities to himself could not be denied as their blood was almost identical. Lunitar's hummed with a power he could not identify and yet recognized within himself. It was foreign and yet so familiar. He had tasted its like when he had created Seth as well, but when he had turned his first, who was of angelic descent, it had not been this way. He never imagined it would be this way again. The connection was undeniable... and it rocked him to the core. He was hesitant to taint another so pure and potent essence, and he almost faltered in his resolve. Then he recognized the familiar gray hue settling into Lunitar's skin and realized there was no turning back. "I gave you my word..." he gasped, half-lost in the power that was inexplicably coursing through his veins. Almost without thought, he sliced his neck open and pulled Lunitar closer.

Lunitar's head rolled back and his mouth opened slightly.

Reivn willed his blood forth from the wound and allowed it to run freely until he grew weak from loss himself. Only then did he draw back and will his wound closed. "You will be the strongest of them," he whispered to the silence.

Knowing he had to get them both to safety from the coming dawn, Reivn carried him from the conservatory and down the hall to his own chambers. "I apologize for your lack of accommodations, my son. When I left here for battle, I did not know I would bring you home. I will see to your quarters tomorrow."

Reivn laid Lunitar on his immense bed and watched over him until the familiar convulsions began. Then he retreated to a chair and sank into its depth in relief. It was done. Now all that was left was to await his transformation.

The day passed in silence and Reivn remained undisturbed in his room. He had slipped into sleep where he sat, his own need for sustenance pushing him into unconsciousness, and he was still there when the sun set again.

When Lunitar awoke, his transformation was complete. Looking around, he marveled at the changes in his perception. There was so much more depth to the world than he had ever imagined. Then he saw Reivn, who was still unconscious and quite pale, and he slid off the bed and hurried over. "Father? Are you all right?" he ventured tentatively. He got no response, so he gently shook Reivn's shoulder.

Reivn finally opened his eyes. "I need to feed..." he groaned.

Lunitar had seen an Immortal in this state before and knew it was dangerous. Worried now, he ran to the door and yanked it open. "Guard!"

Two soldiers on duty in the hall immediately responded. "What's wrong?" one asked. "Where's his lordship?"

"He is in desperate need of sustenance! Bring at least three servants from his herd!" Lunitar's eyes flashed and a glyph appeared on his forehead, as uncontrolled power surged through him.

The guard took a step back in surprise. "Yes... yes sir!" Then he turned and ran down the hall.

The remaining soldier joined Lunitar in the room. "He doesn't look too good," he stated uneasily. "We should move him to the bed."

Lunitar agreed and picked Reivn up. *Is it always like this when you turn someone?* he wondered as he gently carried him to the bed.

The guard returned with three young women in tow. He did not need to instruct them. They quickly went to Reivn and sat down beside him. Then one pulled out a knife, cut her wrist, and pushed it into his mouth.

It was obvious then that this had happened with Reivn before, but the when or why of it was unknown to Lunitar.

Reivn slowly became aware of the blood pouring into his mouth and started to drink, his thirst driving him as need took over.

Finally, the girl needed to pull away.

One of her companions cut her own wrist and held it under Reivn's nose, so he could smell it. He took the bait and grabbed her wrist, letting the first girl go. This time he was more controlled as he slowly regained composure.

Seeing he was going to recover, Lunitar relaxed somewhat. However, he stayed close to ensure no harm befell his benefactor.

The guards eyed him with suspicion. They had felt his power surge but did not trust its origins. They did not know him or why he was here in the first place.

As the third girl was feeding Reivn, he finally became aware of them. He glanced down at the foot of the bed, and when he saw his son, he pushed them away. "Lunitar! You're awake! How do you feel?" He sat up slowly, attempting to disguise the exhaustion he felt.

"Better than you obviously," Lunitar observed, staring at him in concern. "...though I believe your men are somewhat confused. We should probably explain to them who I am."

Reivn glanced past him and realized they had a full room. He frowned at his own lack of discretion. "Guards... go. Announce to all in the Keep there are now three sons belonging to House Draegon."

Both guards snapped to attention, their eyes going wide as they stared at Lunitar. Then after saluting Reivn, they hurried from the room.

The young women beside Reivn quickly bowed to him and scrambled off the bed. Then they bowed to Lunitar and scurried out the door, leaving the two men alone.

"You have no idea exactly how much your life has changed as of yet, and you have much to learn," Reivn began, gazing at Lunitar in earnest. "I can tell you are off to a good start. So, perhaps we shall begin your learning by showing you how to deal with that Glyph..."

# THE BLOODLINE

### Chapter Three
### Hard Lessons

The next few months at Draegonstorm were busy ones for Lunitar and Gideon both. First, they had to master their basic senses and awaken their magic. Then they began to study the Initiate level spells they would need for arena training, and how to summon them quick enough to use in battle.

Reivn worked them hard and showed little mercy in his teachings. His impatience with Gideon was apparent from the start, as was the fact he favored Lunitar. However, Gideon bore it in silence and did not complain.

This odd dynamic was not lost on Lunitar, however, and he wondered more and more what had spawned the strange relationship which had obviously begun long before that fateful night in Mastric's Guild.

The night finally came when Reivn told them he was ready to take their training to the next level. "Lunitar, you will be coming with me to the arena to begin combat training. Gideon, you will remain here and continue your studies with the books on the table. I will be testing you at the end of the week on what you have read, so study them well."

"I am ready to fight too, if you will let me." Gideon argued, frustrated with what he viewed as being held back. "I did learn the sword when..." He fell silent when he saw Reivn's expression.

"I said you will stay here this week. I can only focus on one of you at a time. You will get your chance soon enough." Annoyed now, Reivn turned and walked out the door. "Come, Lunitar. We have work to do."

"Yes, my lord." Lunitar replied and followed him, glancing over his shoulder at Gideon. He felt sorry for him, but he knew Reivn well enough to know better than to argue.

Reivn was quiet as they headed down to the large arena, his mind on Gideon. However, when they arrived his demeanor changed, and he was almost enthusiastic when he turned to Lunitar. "There are many forms of magic to use both on and off the battlefield. Most of them, you can safely practice here. We will also be expanding your knowledge of weaponry and their uses. Which would you like to learn first?"

"Combat magic," Lunitar answered after some reflection. "If I am to stand at your side, I need to do so with confidence and competence."

Reivn chuckled at his expression. "I suspected as much. I have noticed these past few months your thirst for arcane books is nearly insatiable. That is good. The usual training time for a thrall is about seven years, but I do not think it will take you that long. You are stronger than most."

Looking around the arena, Lunitar was curious about the many obstacles that were set up. "Are these all part of the training?"

"They are," Reivn replied. "I will know you are ready for battle when you can navigate these without any mistakes. Be cautious though. They are filled with traps. Part of the training is to learn to detect and safely disarm them. I will change them each week, so you will never know where the attack is coming from."

As he listened, Lunitar realized mastering combat magic was going to be more complicated than he initially thought. He slowly made his way around the perimeter of the arena, carefully inspecting the course.

Watching him with interest, Reivn asked, "What are you looking for?"

"I am not entirely sure," Lunitar answered honestly. "Anything that feels... wrong, because my eyes are telling me one thing, but I believe I now have senses that will tell me the truth." He stopped suddenly and stared at an obstacle, his suspicions rising. "There is one here, isn't there?"

Reivn smiled and walked over to join him. "There is a trap here, yes. And you are right. You do have senses which help with this, but not in the way you think. It is not like your sight, hearing or movement. Those senses are a normal part of every Vampyre. What we as Mastrics were gifted with is far more complex. We can use our birthright to not only sense magic, but to manipulate it as well... some by sheer will alone and others through the language of the Spirals. Like this..." He turned and glanced at the torches on a nearby wall. "Se aprinde!" At his command, they flared to life. "You see?"

"I do... Vocalization provides a necessary frequency to manipulate the energy. Isn't inflection also important, as well as the sequence of syllables?" Lunitar stared at the torch closest to him as he spoke, trying to work out the science behind it in his head.

Reivn nodded. "Correct. The Spirals will not respond to a weak command. You must have the will to control it... " He extinguished the torches and turned to his son. "Try to light them using the same command I did."

Lunitar tried to level all his willpower at the torches, collectively seeing them in his mind. He was determined to succeed. "Se aprinde!" he shouted.

The torches exploded with flames that shot up almost to the ceiling.

Reivn quickly extinguished the fire before it could do any damage. Then he turned with a laugh and said, "Use less enthusiasm for the torches next time. It is only a low level spell."

"Well, in my defense... it was only my first attempt. I will try again." This time, Lunitar turned his focus on only one torch. Concentrating again, he said 'Se aprinde!" This time it was more controlled, and to his surprise it lit perfectly, its light dancing as it reflected on the walls around it.

Reivn chuckled, his expression one of obvious approval. "Well, that was much better. For a moment, I thought your first might be our last. Well done. Now, light the others and let us move on to the next lesson."

Self-examining the difference in how he had cast both times, Lunitar stood silent for a moment, summing up how much willpower he should use. When he was ready, he shifted his glance to the rest of them and cast again. The torches sputtered a moment, and then flickered to life.

Reivn watched in satisfaction. "You are a good student. If only your brother were as astute in learning. However, his talents lie in other areas..." Without finishing his statement, he glanced at the obstacle course. "This is where we work next. I will warn you... you will most likely get injured during this lesson."

Pointing at the scar on his face, Lunitar shrugged. "I'm no stranger to pain. What is one more battle trophy amongst those I already possess?"

"Nothing you sustain here will be permanent,' Reivn reminded him. "I would never do that to you."

His statement surprised Lunitar, who knew how their former master had left scars on all his children when he punished them. "Then the price for the knowledge I acquire is merely pain? Honestly... compared to my previous life, this will be easy then."

Turning to stare at him, Reivn raised an eyebrow. "I thought you knew that scarring only happens if the caster wishes it. Those Mastric bestowed on us as his children and captives were deliberate. What I offer here is merely knowledge. You still have my protection."

"It is greatly appreciated, father." Lunitar bowed respectfully. He was more than ready to master the magic he could feel inside and stared at the course as he spoke, memorizing its layout. "I am eager to be where I can fight at your side, and I am willing to pay whatever price is necessary to ensure I will."

Reivn stood silently milling over his words... critically observing the course with new eyes. He had never wanted to be like his father. Now, as he entered into training his own sons, he realized that he never could be. "Then let us get started..." he replied quietly.

Hearing his tone, Lunitar turned around, his eyes full of understanding. He knew Reivn well enough to realize he would compare his own actions to those of his creator. "I have one request, father. Please do not go easy on me. I wish to master the skills of the Spirals, so I can better perform my duties and exceed my Lord's expectations."

Reivn frowned, wondering if Lunitar thought him weak. "I never go easy on anyone I train," he growled, his eyes beginning to glow with magic, as he prepared to charge the course with power. "Now... do you remember all you have learned thus far about fire spells?"

"I do," Lunitar responded. He shifted his stance to prepare himself for what he knew was coming. "I'm not sure if you're aware of it or not, but I have a perfect memory, and I remember all I read."

Lifting his hands, Reivn blanketed the entire course with magic, awakening the mechanisms that would launch their attacks when triggered. "Good. You will need it. Begin at that end..." He pointed to the far side of the course. "Gradually increase your casting as you progress. I will not tell you where or when to do this. That must be up to you. Use your fire spells to defend yourself from any objects that come at you. Now... begin."

Lunitar went to the starting point and studied the first obstacle carefully for a second before stepping forward. Almost immediately, a barrage of twenty wooden spikes launched at him. He promptly cast a fireball, trying to spread it in front of himself as a barrier. He was not as successful as he hoped. The fireball he created was far smaller than anticipated, and though several spikes were destroyed, one got through and embedded itself in his arm. Wincing from the pain, he paused long enough to test it and see how deep it was. Then seeing it was buried deeper than was safe to remove, he left it and continued on, moving more cautiously.

He approached the second barrier, but nothing happened. Confused, he looked it up and down. Then he lifted his arm and waved slowly in front of the obstacle to test it again. Still nothing. After glancing at Reivn, he finally decided to keep going, thinking the obstacle had been placed without traps to deliberately throw him off. He was wrong. The second he passed it, he heard a click and spun around, bringing his hands up to defend himself. "Seliaprinde!" This time, he tried to make the fireball larger, remembering what Reivn had told him.

More than fifty spikes, these slightly bigger than the last group, flew at him from the rear of the barrier. He managed to throw a large enough spell to destroy most of them, but a couple hit him in the leg and chest. He gasped at the searing pain they inflicted. He had known it would be painful, however, he was not prepared for the extreme agony he felt.

Reivn stood watching Lunitar from the sidelines, and seeing his reaction to the stakes, he explained, "Wood will hurt quite a bit if allowed to embed itself in your chest. The closer to your heart, the more pain it will cause. This is why humans have the legend about stakes. Though one cannot kill us as they believe, it can in fact greatly incapacitate us. Pull out those stakes before you continue."

Wanting them out of his body, Lunitar needed no coaxing. Without hesitation, he withdrew them. The excruciating pain he felt was so foreign to anything he had ever experienced that he almost faltered, and when he was done, he had to pause to catch his breath before continuing on.

Reivn was not done with him yet. "Now... focus on your wounds and close them. This is an important skill you will need on the battlefield."

Lunitar looked up in confusion. "I thought the Clerics heal the wounded," he stated.

"They do," Reivn answered, understanding his confusion. "However, if there are no clerics around, learning this could make a difference in your ability to survive."

Recognizing the sense in what he said, Lunitar obediently closed his eyes and focused on his wounds. To his surprise, he could see them in his head. So he reached out mentally, trying to envision them closing. Nothing happened. Then he heard Reivn's voice in his mind.

*Focus on one wound at a time. This is a much harder task for you than it once was for me. You were not turned with the ability to do so, but it is a skill you absolutely must learn if you are to survive. Now... try again.*

Lunitar followed his guidance and focused on the hole in his chest first. When it slowly began to close, however, he felt an immense drain of energy. He ignored it, choosing to continue as his father instructed. By the time he got to the third injury, he was beginning to feel exhausted.

"Stop!" Reivn commanded, as though he had been waiting for this moment.

Lunitar opened his eyes immediately, wondering if he had done something wrong.

Reivn had halted the magic on the obstacle course and was walking toward him. "Do you feel it?" he asked. "...the weight?"

"Yes, I do," Lunitar replied, somewhat confused. "It is much harder to do than the fire spells, and it takes twice as much effort. I feel as though I have been fighting in battle for hours."

Nodding in understanding, Reivn turned and waved to a girl who had entered the arena at some point without Lunitar's notice. "I wanted you to understand the dangers of taxing yourself too hard. Remember this. When you are trying to heal yourself, only choose the worst of your wounds and leave those that are survivable to the Clerics." He stepped aside for the healer, so she could see to Lunitar's injuries. "You are done for the night. You need time to recover. We will do more tomorrow. First, let's see to those wounds and get you fed."

"Yes, my Lord." Lunitar was silent as he thought about the lesson. Then he said, "Father... may I ask a question?"

Reivn turned around. "Of course."

"Why is healing so difficult? You said you were once able to, but that it is no longer... available. Why?" Lunitar was understandably confused.

Reivn stood there for a moment, unsure how to explain to his son what had actually happened all those years ago. Finally, he replied, "It is not something I can discuss at this time. All I will tell you is it was Mastric's decision. The Clerics do the healing, which leaves us free to fight our enemies." He looked as if he were about to say something more, but then he changed his mind and fell silent.

"I understand." Lunitar knew better than to ask further questions where Mastric was involved. He knew that sooner or later he would learn the truth, but this was a subject best left alone for now.

The Cleric finished closing Lunitar's wounds, and then bowed and scurried away as silently as she had come.

Reivn waited until they were alone. Then he whispered, "There are some things we just cannot discuss. In time, you will learn much. However, that time cannot be now. Forgive me."

Lunitar nodded and glanced again at the course, wondering how much more difficult it would be in the nights to come. "There is nothing to forgive, father. I promise I will not disappoint you."

"I know," Reivn replied quietly. "Now, come. You still need to feed."

The familiar revulsion Lunitar felt at the thought of the process he was slowly growing accustomed to filled his thoughts, but he obediently followed Reivn from the arena. As they walked, he tried to focus on his learning instead, mulling over that night's lessons. "Father, if I may..."

Reivn glanced sideways at him. "You can always ask questions, my son. That is one thing I want to make perfectly clear. Our dynamics have changed in relationship and rank only. I still hold the value of knowledge above all things. So, ask what you must. I will do my best to answer."

Lunitar nodded, and then said, "In the obstacle course, I chose to use a fireball for my first tactic and noticed it wasn't large enough. So, I tried to enlarge it by spreading it out. Would it have been wiser to use it as a tower shield so as to more completely protect myself?"

Reivn smiled, evidently pleased by the question. "You already think like a warrior who uses magic on the battlefield as much as he does weapons. Yes... using fire as a shield is wise. Your lack of execution was not in your idea but rather in your choice of words during casting. The combinations we use when speaking the language of the Spirals determines both the volume and strength of the spell. Whereas a one word combination works for something as simple as a fireball, you need something more complex when creating a shield wall."

This explanation surprised Lunitar and he walked along in silence, working it out in his head. Finally, he said, "So, we are limited not as much by the power we contain, as we are by our own knowledge in the manipulation of that power. Then would it not be possible to erect a shield of intense heat around or in front of you? Not necessarily in a physical manifestation... more like heat that radiates from a volcano. That way, your vision is not obscured, but the magic would still be effective in eliminating the threat, which in this case was the wood spikes."

Reivn chuckled at his enthusiasm. "You are a quick study. I like that. However, a heat shield is not necessary. We have other spells that create shields of a more kinetic nature. They are more complicated than the spells you are learning right now. As you rise in the ranks from novice to a Master of the arcane, spells like those will become second nature."

Lunitar listened with interest, fascinated by all he was learning. He was surprised at how much was kept from the servants in Mastric's care. "So, are there different levels in both ranks and spells, or just in ranks, where you learn more complex spells?"

Reivn stopped and looked at him. "I see why he was reluctant to let me have you. You are very perceptive." He paused for a second. "There are multiple levels in both ranks and spells," he explained. "With spells, there are eight recognized levels of various kinds, and these each fall into one of twelve categories. As for ranks, there are eight of those as well, and you only progress from one to the next after you have mastered all the spells in each of the categories for your rank's achievement range."

Lunitar sighed in frustration. "I hope to progress far faster than other novices. That is my goal, you know."

"How could I not know," Reivn smiled. "You are as inquisitive as any human child, and you absorb everything you are taught like a sponge. Ah, here we are. Your quarters, I believe. I will leave you here. Summon a servant to feed on before you retire. That is not a request, either. I understand your aversion, as it was once my own, but you will get used to it in time."

"I had hoped you would not notice my struggle with that aspect of our existence," Lunitar stated bluntly. "I am trying, but it is definitely an adjustment. Still... I will do as you command, father."

Reivn rested a hand on his shoulder. "Remember this. You will grow weak if you do not feed, and in the trials ahead, the lessons will not be easy. They will weaken you enough when you have fed well. If you have not fed at all, they could in fact kill you. I will not allow that, so see to your needs."

Lunitar watched him walk away in silence, knowing he was right. His frustration with himself was growing. He felt he could do far better than he presently was in his magic, but the key to it still evaded him. After standing there thinking for a few minutes, he finally turned his footsteps to the library instead of his room. "If I am going to succeed, then there is something I really need to do."

When Lunitar finally returned from the library shortly before dawn, his arms were loaded with books. He pushed his door open, intent on setting them down and getting to reading. He came face to face with a young woman. "From my father, I presume?" he asked her graciously, exuding more self-control than he felt at the slight intrusion.

"Yes, my Lord," she answered politely. "I am to see to your needs before you sleep."

In frustration, he put the books down and walked over to her. He knew there was no avoiding it, and he wanted it done with so he could get to his studies. "Very well. I should have realized he would send someone."

In response, she merely bared her neck to him.

He took her wrist instead, firmly gripping it to prevent any movement which could cause her injury. Then he sank his fangs in and began to drink. He closed his eyes, letting the coppery fluid do its job rejuvenating him, while he tried to shut out her thoughts and emotions. He hated having to feel their fear each time he fed. He understood it was because he was young. They were afraid he would have a lack of control that could end them, but it still irritated him. He could never hurt anyone that way. He understood all too well their position as servants. So he drank what he needed and immediately closed her wound. "Now... leave me," he stated more than asked as he turned his back on her and reached for the books again.

She was surprised. She had expected he would want to taste of her additional talents as others did, but he was apparently more interested in the tomes he had brought than he was in her. She hesitated for a moment longer before finally getting up and quietly leaving his room.

If he noticed her exit, he did not show it, as he continued to search through the books he had brought with him until he found what he was looking for. Then he settled back on his bed and began to read.

## Chapter Four
## Guild's Cage

Seth awoke to strange surroundings, dark and cold. Almost immediately, waves of pain flooded his senses, and he rolled onto his side, vomiting blood over the edge of the bed. His body felt as though it had been rent limb from limb.

"Rest easy. Severing a blood tie between father and son does have rather nasty side-effects, I am afraid." Mastric stepped from the shadows into the light of the torches. "Your training begins now. Your first lesson is to swear absolute obedience to me. If you do not, what you are experiencing now is but a shadow to what awaits you."

His stomach still twisting in knots, Seth gasped for air between heaves, his eyes blurring as he glanced up at the ominous figure who stood beside him. "Why..." was all he managed to choke out before launching into another round.

Mastric smiled beneath his hood and stared down at him. "I am your father's maker, and now... your Master."

Dropping back on the bed as his innards finally began to settle, Seth realized he was naked. He gazed up at his captor in loathing. "Why?" he repeated. His eyes demanded an answer.

Deciding to humor the man, who obviously had no idea who he was speaking to, Mastric chuckled. "Your father made you without first consulting me. This is his punishment more so than yours. You were merely a bonus. Understand that you have no choice in this. All who are of this tribe are subject to my will. Now, get up and kneel before me. Give me your word of obedience and I will allow you to move about freely while you learn."

Seth slowly got up, fighting back the urge to retch again. He realized Reivn was gone, and any connection he had to him had been stripped away. So, he dropped to his knees, wary of the cruel Ancient in front of him. Then he bowed his head to the floor. "I will serve you..."

Mastric eyed him for a minute, clearly pleased with his new toy. Seth was young, and it would be many years before he had any real use of his abilities. So there was no point in binding him. "Rest tonight. I will send for you at dusk tomorrow and we will begin your lessons," he instructed. Then he turned away and drifted to the door.

Seth got to his feet and watched him go. He was under no illusions concerning his situation. *I need to find my way out of here tonight and try to get back to Reivn. Then we can figure out what to do next. I'm sure that together, we can defeat this bastard.* He began searching the room for anything that would help him, but little other than clothing had been provided. The rest of the room was bare. His armor was gone, and so were his weapons.

Ruffling through the clothes offered, he finally settled on all black, and slipped on pants and a simple shirt. Then he pulled on boots and donned a heavy cloak. When he was done, he did not hesitate. He went to the door and cracked it open, cautiously peering into the gloom beyond.

The hall was empty.

Seth slipped into the corridor in total silence, thankful Reivn had taught him how to use his Immortal senses. Keeping his eyes and ears trained on his surroundings, he crept toward the stairwell at the end of the hall. He did not know where he was, but he knew from Reivn's descriptions of the Guild that he had to be underground. That meant going up. So, when he reached the stairwell, he climbed them quickly. *So far, so good,* he thought. Once upstairs, he moved swiftly through the Guild, searching for the exit. He knew once he was out, he would have to travel fast to put distance between himself and his captor before dawn.

When Seth reached the front hall, he cautiously looked around, wondering why there were no guards. *Had this been my stronghold, I would have men standing watch, magic or no magic.* Then he shook his head at the apparent lack of security, all the while thanking his luck. He hurried across the entryway and was almost to the doors when a voice behind him stopped him in his tracks.

"Now where are you going in such a hurry?"

Seth straightened up and turned around slowly. It was not a voice he recognized.

Valfort stood leaning casually against the wall with his arms crossed.

Eyeing him carefully, Seth inched toward the door, trying not to make it obvious. "Who are you?" he asked casually, trying to keep the edginess from his voice.

With a laugh, Valfort stated, "I'm the guard you obviously thought was absent. You're too young to know this, so I will spell it out for you. I am a Warlord, or to be more precise, the Warlord for the Mastrics tribe. I do not believe you have permission to leave here."

Turning to face him fully, Seth drew to a halt. "You do not know what I can or cannot do, and I do not answer to you. For all you know, I was given orders to go somewhere. No rank is infallible. Even you must answer to your lord."

"You're right. I do," Valfort sneered. "And he is right behind you."

Seth spun around just in time to be lifted into the air by Mastric's magic. "Let me go..." he choked out.

Mastric grinned from beneath his hood. "So brazen for a whelp. That's good. It means you have the will to survive your training. And since you are apparently fully recovered, there is no time like the present to begin." He dropped Seth to the floor and turned away. "Bring him."

Seth gasped for air and struggled to his feet, intent on making a run for the door.

Valfort was at his side in the blink of an eye and grabbed him by his hair. Then following Mastric, he dragged the struggling man down the hall. "Come on, dog. Time to put on your collar."

"Let go of me!" Seth snarled, fighting to free himself. But his efforts were futile against the Elder. He could only stare hopelessly at the doors that would have given him freedom until they disappeared from sight.

Mastric was seething with anger. *He will learn to bow his head to me, or I will crush the life from him.* He waved his hand, and the door to his lab opened. Then he floated into the room and over to a set of shelves on the wall.

Valfort followed, dragging Seth behind him. He dumped his captive on the floor at Mastric's feet.

"Leave us!" Mastric commanded, staring down at Seth in cold, calculated fury.

Bowing low, Valfort backed from the room. He was not going to challenge Mastric's will when he was in such a foul mood. His eyes lingered a moment on Seth before he closed the door and he smiled. *Enjoy your night, boy...* he telepathied. Then he left them alone.

Mastric raised his hand, levitating Seth to a standing position. "I'm going to assume you are either a fool or you have a death wish!" he snarled.

Seth turned red as his temper flared. "I must see Reivn! He honored me by saving my life! I will not just abandon him!"

"Do you think me a fool?" Mastric roared. With a thought, he sent Seth flying into the far wall, where invisible chains captured and restrained him. Then the master of magic levitated over to hover in front of him. "I cannot decide if you are overly brave or just too stupid to realize the truth of your circumstances! If you think Reivn is all-powerful, then you must know I am a God! I can crush you both with a single thought! You have entered a world where obedience is the law! I was prepared to be lenient with you since you were a victim of circumstance, but now you will know the full measure of what it is that possesses you!" He drew closer to the young man and growled. "I am your worst nightmare and the monster in the dark you fear!"

Raising his chin proudly, Seth stared at him boldly, refusing to show fear. "I am a Northman! I have fought in battle and faced death a thousand times. I do not fear it! Kill me and I will join my brothers in Valhalla."

Mastric laughed at him, amused by his shortsighted bravery. "No, child. You will be here a long time. I have no intention of letting you go. I know you Norsemen are fearless in battle, so I have many uses for a warrior like you." He waved and Seth's hand was immediately yanked up and restrained. An iron spike flew across the room and slammed into the Northman's wrist, nailing him to the wall behind.

Seth gritted his teeth, refusing to yell. Beads of bloody sweat ran down his face as he forced himself to keep silent.

Mastric was not done. In mere seconds, another spike had pinned Seth's other wrist as well, crucifying him. Then he floated back to the ground, and his voice echoed with sheer, raw power. "Seliaputre Arovite Na Aprinde Nochorem!" As he spoke, the flames of wrath wrapped around Seth, licking at his skin with ferocity.

Seth's eyes widened as the sheer agony hit him. *This is no warrior's death. He's burning me as an animal sacrifice!* He thought in a panic.

"No, child," Mastric answered, listening in on his thoughts. "Those flames will not damage one hair on your body. Since you are brave enough to suffer through punishment, let's see how well you embrace a few weeks on my wall with only the flames for company." He turned to leave, and then said over his shoulder. "Sleep well."

His refusal to yield born of his heritage, Seth closed his eyes, forcing himself to accept the pain. He had no idea how long he could endure it, but he would as long as his will held out.

Hours ticked by... then nights, weeks, and months, and eventually Seth had no recollection of how much time had passed. He had long since ceased to fight and had succumbed to the agony, hanging listless and half-conscious as the flames of wrath continued to torment him. No one visited him, and the room was devoid of any light save for the purple hue engulfing his body. All hope of escape or rescue was gone.

## Chapter Five
## Graduation Night

First months, then years flew by for Lunitar and Gideon, as Reivn worked them relentlessly in their training. They had to master the obstacle courses and spent endless hours of study in the library. Then it was more practice with weapons and combat on the training grounds, until finally, the day came when he took them to the arena to test their skills. It was time to see if they could use all they had learned in battle.

Lunitar stood off to the side, watching as his father quietly talked with the men who would oppose them. The arena was filling up quickly with spectators, both from Draegonstorm and the Guilds around Europe, who wanted to see how Reivn's sons would fare in their greatest trial. He was under no illusion how difficult the night ahead was going to be.

Gideon was leaning against the wall in brooding silence, staring across the expanse at his father. He had heard rumors as to what was supposed to transpire in these tests. He glanced at Lunitar and sighed. *Has father told you what is supposed to happen tonight?* he telepathied, wondering if his brother knew more about the impending trial than he did.

*No, he has not. Focus on the objective and let your emotions go,* Lunitar sent back, eyeing the group that was prepping for the battle with interest. There were at least a hundred men.

Walking over to stand by his brother, Gideon motioned toward them. "You do know they are supposed to try and kill us?"

Lunitar turned and gazed at him steadily. "They will try... Remember Gideon... action is faster than reaction, and your emotions will slow your actions." He put his hand on his brother's shoulder.

Anything further he could have said was cut short as Reivn joined them. "Everything is ready," he stated. "Here are the rules. You must use everything you have learned and fight until you are either killed or manage to injure all of them enough to incapacitate them. Only then will we know you are ready to join us in the war." He started to walk away, but then he paused and looked at Lunitar. "I know this is brutal... some would even say barbaric. However, the way the Principatus fights is far worse than anything you will see here tonight."

"It will be what it must, father," Lunitar answered, bowing his head slightly. He could see the worry in Reivn's eyes and knew he wanted this even less than they did.

Gideon stared at his father as he walked away, the hurt in his eyes apparent. Reivn had spoken to Lunitar, but not to him. "Father! What happens if we kill one of your men?" he called after a second.

Reivn turned around again, gazing him coldly. "You need not worry. I have Clerics here to prevent that from happening. Still... it would mean you actually managed to learn a thing or two during your training."

Stung by the sharp rebuttal, Gideon fell silent and dropped his gaze. "I learned just as much as my brother," he murmured to himself.

"We shall see..." Reivn responded immediately.

Lunitar gazed from one to the other, long since used to the hostilities between them, but it still concerned him. He was about to telepathy Gideon to reassure him, when Reivn began to announce the trial's commencement.

Reivn walked around the outer edge of the arena, explaining the ground rules for everyone to hear. Finally, he turned and glanced at his sons, his eyes briefly meeting Lunitar's before yelling "Begin!"

Immediately, the one hundred warriors on the far side of the field spread out and charged.

Lunitar had armed himself with a long sword and main gauche, and as he walked forward, he drew them both. He carefully studied which direction his opponents were going and prepared to engage them.

Gideon had also sprung into action. Armed with a blade in one hand, he quickly cast a shield with his other. Then seeing that Lunitar had not yet done so, he quickly telepathied, *Lunitar... put up your shield!*

Lunitar did not respond. Completely focused on their opponents, he had circled sideways, refusing to let them flank him. Then he concentrated his magic into a crescent-shaped kinetic shield to guard his back. Now he looked for the best opportunity to engage his attackers.

Gideon had circled around in the opposite direction, and their attackers had moved between them. However, they were spread wide, making any mass attack extremely unlikely.

When Lunitar closed to about fifteen feet from their adversaries, he opened his mind and sent out a telepathic scream, putting as much force behind it as possible. It rippled across the entire arena in a psionic wave that battered the senses of anyone mentally unprotected.

Many of the onlookers closed their eyes, groaning as pain hit their senses and momentarily disoriented them.

A handful of their opponents faltered as pain hit them and disoriented them. Still, most of them had been ready for it and stood their ground, wondering what other tricks the Mastric's warriors would try.

Stumbling sideways, Gideon tried to shake off the effects of his brother's telepathic assault. He had not expected it, and his head was reeling. He tried to focus his sight on their attackers, knowing he was vulnerable, and then summoned a firestorm and unleashed it directly in front of him, hoping to deflect a full assault until his vision cleared.

Soldiers scrambled to grab their stunned comrades and dive out of the way of the flames, but they were quick to recover. Almost immediately, several moved in from Gideon's left, weapons brandished.

Lunitar closed the distance between himself and a few who were stunned by his attack, immediately engaging them. He quickly found himself fighting multiple opponents, as their fellow soldiers jumped to their defense, and the ringing of blades filled the air.

Gideon managed to deflect the first attackers, even though his sight had not yet fully returned. He used his other senses to compensate, gauging their locations by sound and smell until he could see again. Annoyed with Lunitar, he momentarily glared across the arena, believing his brother had tried to sabotage him. However, there was no time for him to dwell on that thought, as more of their opponents moved in. Now they were attacking from all sides, forcing him to the defensive.

Shouts rang out as they tried to route the two young Mastrics and keep them apart. On both sides now, it was a full-on battle. Then out of nowhere, bolts of kinetic energy came streaking down toward them.

Lunitar ducked and rolled immediately, seeking to avoid the blasts of magic. Then he spun around, trying to identify their source.

Reivn stood to one side of the arena, casting magic and pelting the field with it as he watched the battle.

Gideon bolstered his shield and shaped it to deflect the bolts toward their attackers. Once they hit and bounced off, he changed position to avoid becoming a target again.

Lunitar quickly sought a way to even the odds and grabbed the nearest assailant to use as a shield from the magical barrage. He quickly realized Reivn was simulating the attacks Daemons would use in battle. So he tried to compensate by wading deeper into their ranks, knowing the magic would hit some of them as well. All over the field, Reivn's attacks rained down on the scattered soldiers, causing total chaos in their wake.

Weaving in and out among his opponents, Gideon attacked again, taking out as many as possible while they were distracted.

Lunitar wanted this over and done with. He continued fighting, but he was using the flat of his blade to incapacitate them rather than the sharpened edge.

Without warning, a group of archers joined the battle, quickly lining the arena's edge and kneeling as they nocked their arrows. Then with a nod from Reivn, they fired on the fighting men.

Gideon did not see their flying arrows and jumped back in shock when one hit the man in front of him. Then he looked over and his eyes widened.

From his vantage point, Lunitar also spotted the archers, but he was too engaged to directly avoid the arrows raining down on top of him and those around him. He quickly grabbed the nearest soldier to use as a shield. The man caught five that would have hit him. Trying not to think about that, he dropped the soldier and moved on.

Their opponents turned on them with a vengeance, and Gideon found himself engaged on all sides, turning with every blow he managed to deflect. His shield was beginning to flicker, as he pushed his magic to the limit, and it was obvious he was tiring.

Lunitar found himself getting swarmed as well, engaged by multiple attackers, as arrows continued to fall all around them.

Then fire began to hit the ground and explode all around them. Reivn had switched tactics and let lose a firestorm above them. Mimicking Hellfire, he winced when he saw the damage it was doing.

A fireball slammed into Lunitar's shoulder as he defended himself from several swordsmen moving at blurring speeds. With sudden terrifying and blinding pain, it washed down across him like molten lava, momentarily causing him to stumble. His opponents reacted by increasing their attacks and going in for the kill. Then somewhere deep inside him something snapped, and he screamed in pure rage. His eyes shifted to a deep blue and the glyph on his forehead became visible with blinding brilliance. He turned his blades, increased his speed and tore into his opponents mercilessly as one objective filled his mind: kill or be killed.

On the sidelines, a third contingent of one hundred soldiers arrived and prepared to join the battle. As their comrades fell one after another, they quickly jumped in and replaced them.

Reivn watched Lunitar with knowing eyes. He recognized that look and realized his son had crossed the threshold and was no longer holding back. *Remarkable. They are facing a full company and are still fighting. It took five full platoons, but he has finally hit his rage... Now we will see what he can do...*

On the other side of the field, Gideon fell to his knees. His strength failed, and his shield was gone. Now he struggled to catch his breath, as he snapped off the shafts of two arrows protruding from his chest. Then yelling in pain, he forced himself to his feet, desperate to prove he was worthy of his freedom. He drove into the soldiers around him in almost blind rage as he fought them off.

All around them, the attacking soldiers moved with the finesse and blurring speed the Mithranian tribe was known for, pushing both Mastrics to the limits of their abilities. Each time they closed in and dodged away again, they came closer to scoring a vital hit on first one then the other of Reivn's sons.

Lunitar started inching his way toward Gideon. His arms ached, and the flesh on his shoulder and upper torso burned with seething pain from his wounds, making it difficult for him to focus. So to give himself an edge, he quickly summoned molten flames and blanketed his sword in them. Then he pushed on, moving at blinding speed, as he engaged his opponents.

The field was covered with injured men, arrows, and small clusters of flames that burned around them. Clerics worked at its edge, pulling out the wounded and healing their injuries, while more soldiers took their place. Arrows continued to rain down on the chaotic exchange, mingled with the repeated firestorms that were taking a serious toll on both sides.

A soldier landed a blow on Gideon's shoulder, crushing his collarbone, and he screamed in anguish. Tears streaming down his face, he kept fighting, refusing to give in. Swinging his blade with his good arm in desperation, he cut a path toward Lunitar. He knew his only chance now was to fight side by side with his brother.

Hearing his brother's cry, Lunitar quickly looked for him. Then he pushed at the wall of men surrounding him. However, their opponent's numbers were holding, and no matter how many he cut down, they just kept coming. Desperate to get to Gideon before it was too late, he closed his eyes and reached deep into himself... searching for more power.

His adversaries saw him pause and immediately attacked. Their blades hit empty space.

Lunitar had vanished.

The soldiers spun around in confusion... perplexed by his sudden disappearance.

In seconds, however, he reappeared beside Gideon. He dropped his shield and immediately put his back to his brother's. Then he tore into the men surrounding them with renewed vengeance.

Gideon was shocked by his brother's sudden appearance and it took him a second to realize what had happened. Then seeing Lunitar's determination, he steadied himself and renewed his efforts.

Reivn briefly closed his eyes, breathing a sigh of relief. He could see the flood gates opening for Lunitar with his magic and knew he would pass the test. Then his gaze fell on Gideon. Though still standing, the youth had quite a few injuries, and had spent what magic he could use. *He is not yet ready to be released from thralldom, but he may still be able to fight in a lower ranked capacity*, he concluded.

Neither side was yielding, and Reivn recognized the battle had come to a stalemate. He knew it was finally time to bring the test to its conclusion. One last blast of magic would confirm or deny what he was seeing here. He raised his hands and began to cast. The pop of electricity filled his fingertips and grew to staggering proportions. Almost instantaneously, lightning began to streak through the air above the fighting mass. He drew on it, further charging his power. Then he unleashed it, launching bolts of lightning in every direction.

Shouts rang out as the Mastric soldiers who could, immediately raised kinetic shields around themselves and their comrades.

Those who could not raise a shield ducked for cover and tried to avoid the deadly bolts that were swiftly taking over the entire battlefield.

When Lunitar saw it, he knew it was far more powerful than any of the previous attacks. These were enough to kill anyone in their path. So using everything he had, he raised the biggest shield he could summon and covered as many soldiers as possible, unwilling to let any who were not truly his enemies die.

Gideon understood at a glance and joined him, casting one last shield of his own and expanding it to meet his brother's.

Seeing their decision to protect the men they knew to be allies, Reivn nodded in satisfaction. They had passed the final segment of the test... teamwork and a willingness to defend the innocent, even at personal cost. They were ready. He stopped his barrage of lightning and shouted across the field, "Enough!"

The soldiers lowered their weapons immediately, realizing the trial was finally over. One by one, they began leaving the arena, some with help from their comrades to the waiting arms of Clerics.

Gideon dropped his blade where he stood and sank to his knees in exhaustion.

Lunitar chose to remain standing and turned to gaze across the field at his father, waiting for his next command.

Reivn patiently waited for the wounded to be taken care of, knowing some of his men were in need of immediate care.

When Lunitar saw his father was dealing with the wounded first, he turned to find Gideon. Seeing his brother on his knees, he sheathed his sword and closed the distance between them. Then he offered him a hand. "Come, Gideon. Get to your feet. It's over." He was breathing heavily, the pain he felt coming in waves now that his adrenaline had dissipated.

Gideon slowly rose, wincing from the pain, and gazed at Lunitar with new respect. His brother had out-performed him in every way, and he knew it. "Thank you," he whispered humbly. He knew in his heart he had not met his father's expectations.

"You are welcome, but you do not have to thank family," Lunitar replied quietly. "You are my brother, and if need be, I would die for you."

Reivn approached and overheard his last remark. "If he were worthy of such, that would be commendable. However, he has a long way to go before he can claim that kind of value." He stared at Gideon in obvious disapproval. "You wasted your magic in the opening. You stayed on the defensive and refused to actually attack your adversaries until your life was at serious risk. If our other warriors fought that way, we would not live very long, and the Principatus would run rampant in the territories."

Gideon lowered his gaze in shame. "Forgive me father. Though I learned to use a sword, I have never actually seen battle until now. I was unsure how to proceed. Our training taught us logistics, but not practical application. I will not disappoint you again."

Instead of responding, Reivn turned to Lunitar and his demeanor immediately changed. "I was impressed by your performance in the arena. You did not waste your magic, instead conserving it for when it was needed most. You adapted to the changes in battle and used not only your surroundings to defend yourself, but your wits as well. However, you showed compassion to your enemies in the beginning, defending those around you by using the flat of your blade until you were wounded. Why?"

Lunitar was silent as he digested his father's words. Then he replied, "Because these men are our allies. Had we been in an actual battle with real enemies, I would have started with my blade's edge. As you well know, I am no stranger to war. Once I realized you would keep putting more men in front of me until I treated this as a real battle, I knew I was only delaying the inevitable. However, I am curious about one thing."

"And that is?" Reivn gazed at him expectantly, waiting for the answer.

Motioning toward the men being treated by clerics, Lunitar asked, "Aren't some of them Mastrics?"

Reivn leaned over and picked up one of the weapons from the ground, understanding immediately where he was going. "Some of them were."

Lunitar frowned. "Then why wouldn't they use their magic to attack, or at the very least, defend themselves?"

"Because I ordered them not to," Reivn replied, walking over to hand the weapon to one of his guards. "The Principatus wins battles by throwing hordes at us. Numbers, Lunitar... in the thousands. The only magic they have is what a select few can conjure from Tartarus, and though powerful, with enough Mastrics on the field, we can defend from that most of the time. So it is not magic you need to worry about nearly so much as the thousands that will just keep coming no matter how many you kill. This is their primary tactic, and it has cost us many battles. All our power combined is no match for the endless numbers that frequently overwhelm us. We still tire, and they exploit that fact." He paused and glanced around to be sure no one was within earshot other than his sons. "There is one more thing I noticed concerning your performance tonight... the change in you when you were injured. I have seen that look before."

Dropping his gaze and shifting uncomfortably, Lunitar cleared his throat before replying, "It was the primal urge to survive, and honestly, my restraint slipped. I momentarily stepped back into the man you saved me from.... the monster I used to be."

Reivn frowned at his confession. "You were never the monster..." he whispered. "However, that is a discussion for another time. Go and get your wounds seen to, and then come see me in my office." Then he glanced once more at Gideon. "Get your wounds seen to as well and take the rest of the night to rest. We will talk tomorrow."

They both bowed. "As you command, my lord," they said almost in unison. Then they watched him walk away before heading over to join the other soldiers who were being cared for at the arena's edge.

## Chapter Six
## Dragon's Heir

Gideon knew he had failed and chastised himself for it. He walked over and sat by himself to wait until one of the Clerics were free to heal him. He wanted to be alone. *How am I supposed to prove to him that I am not the same person he met all those years ago? If he doesn't want me here, then why keep me in the first place?* After a few minutes, he glanced over at Lunitar, wondering how his brother felt about the test they had just endured. He had long since recognized the bond his father and brother shared and was curious how they had met.

Lunitar was busy self-analyzing his performance, picking apart how he could improve. He stared down at the damage to his hands and arms, wondering why the use of magic had burned him so badly. Then he remembered the sudden teleport he had managed. *I knew it was possible, but I haven't studied that spell. Was it need-driven or did I just get lucky? Is all this damage from me reaching too far? Maybe they're connected...* He was certain now that there was a possibility of reaching beyond one's capabilities and suffering serious consequences... perhaps even death.

A Cleric approached Lunitar, disrupting his thoughts. "My lord... I was ordered to see to your wounds. Will you allow me?"

He looked around. "Are all the critically injured already seen to? If not, I can wait."

Surprised by his question, she shook her head. "My lord, I was ordered to heal you. The others are handling them. However, your wounds are different and require my skill. So Lord Reivn sent me here to tend you."

"How are my wounds any different from theirs? We were in the same battle." He gazed down at her in curiosity.

The girl looked up at him in astonishment. "I am referring to your wounds from using too much magic. When we are relatively new to the blood, our bodies can only channel what we have grown to learn. This is why we constantly practice and stretch the limits of our capabilities... to slowly acclimate to the use of more magic. The longer one of us has been a Mastric, the more powerful we grow, depending on our descendancy from the master. When we push too hard, those burns are the result."

"Or they are the warning that we are at our limit," he replied. "Something to consider."

She giggled slightly at his response. "No sir. We are Mastrics. There is no limit to what we can learn... only how much we can use in repeated succession during one battle because even though our bodies are conduits for the Spirals, we also burn through our blood when we use them. That is what actually weakens us. You will no doubt need to feed and rest when we are finished here."

Lunitar held out his hands as they spoke, so she could begin focusing on her work. "I was referring to the fact that we as the conduit are the limiting factor, and these burns a warning we have pushed too far. So, no Mastric should walk away from a pitched battle unburned."

Glancing up at him, her eyes filled with worry. "That is not the way it is done, my lord. Mastric warriors are trained to use their magic to merely compliment their skills in combat, defending themselves with magic only in dire need, but they never extend themselves that far unless in absolute necessity. The Principatus has no magic of their own... only that which they wield through Daemons."

Confused by the idea a Mastric should restrain themselves in battle, he asked, "If we are on the verge of losing a battle and are holding back our magic to preserve our strength, could we not possibly win that fight if we commit what strength we have? And could it not also reduce the casualties we suffer?"

"Sir, we have many varied tribes who fight side by side on the front lines," she explained, briefly glancing up as she worked. "The Mastrics are the only ones who have such command of magic. The Thylacinians and Mithranians are masters at war, and as such are always the ones to lead the battles, but the Mastrics are among the most valued of the tribes, because we possess arcane knowledge no one else has access to. If we all burned all we have, then the Alliance would lose their most valuable asset... magic. It is for this reason that Mastrics are so harshly trained before being allowed to fight. It is to guarantee they understand their threshold." She finished healing the majority of his wounds, and then let go of him. "The rest of your burns will heal in a week or two. I have done all I can." Then she turned to go.

"Before you go... what is your name?" he asked.

She looked back over her shoulder and smiled. "My name is Rebecca. Good luck to you, my lord."

"Thank you, Rebecca," he said as she walked away.

Lunitar headed to his father's office, his mind on what she had said.

Reivn looked up when he entered, his eyes drifting to his son's hands. "You certainly look better than you did earlier. How do you feel?"

"After Rebecca's ministrations, much better, father. However, she has enlightened me on some things I must think about and at some point, discuss with you, once I figure out what I want to ask."

Nodding in understanding, Reivn motioned for him to sit down. "You did well tonight," he observed. "I know you are ready to fight, and it is probably a good thing. I received word from Mastric that I am to join him in a visit to the Council. There is a difficult mission ahead, and they are only sending the first Elders this time." He paused and set aside the letter he was working on. "Before I leave, we have two things to do. However, you need to feed again first. You are a little too weak at the moment. Come." He held up his arm and opened his wrist.

Lunitar accepted without complaint, drinking what he needed. It did not escape his notice that Reivn was still at full strength, even after having expended so much magic... and he had no burns.

Reivn waited silently until Lunitar was done. Then he closed his wound and sat back. "How do you feel now?" he asked quietly.

"Honestly, father, I feel better now than I did when I went into battle," Lunitar admitted. He was slightly confused by this fact.

"I am glad to hear it," Reivn replied somberly. "Then you are ready." He paused for a second and then stood up invoking his blood. "As Lord of Draegonstorm and progenitor of our bloodline, I release you from thralldom."

Lunitar was immediately engulfed in bluish white flames. He gasped as both power and pain flooded his senses, and his knees buckled. He hit the floor hard, the unbridled and unrestrained flow of the full measure of the Spirals pounding at him like waves against the cliffs. Convulsing on the floor, he finally screamed. His glyph glowed in brilliant blue radiance as the power coursed through him, completing the cycle of his turning. Long minutes passed until the pain finally began to subside. Shaking from the strain, he could only manage to pull himself up on all fours, and then hovered there trying to get his bearings.

Reivn waited in silence. His thoughts raced to the nights ahead, and he stared at the letter in front of him.

Finally, Lunitar was able to get up, but he was shaking from head to toe, as his body struggled to absorb the immense amount of power that had become a part of him. "It is done. I am finally ready to fight at your side. Know that none shall harm you as long as I still stand."

Looking up, Reivn gazed at him through a veiled expression, unwilling to show the relief he felt at hearing Lunitar's enthusiasm. His own fears alleviated, he turned his attention to the second subject he needed to broach. "Then you are feeling all right?" he asked tentatively. "I know all too well how painful that was. Are you up to stepping into your duties now? Or do you need time to rest?"

"No rest for the weary. If there are duties needing attention, then I will do my part to help." Lunitar straightened himself up and smiled. "I'll rest when I'm dead."

With a nod, Reivn walked over to stand beside him. "Then kneel."

Lunitar knelt on his left knee and bowed his head.

"I name you my heir and my second here at Draegonstorm now and for all time. I also commission you to military service in the Honor Guard. You will take command of the fortress in my pending absence." Reivn rested his hand on Lunitar's shoulder. "You fight at my side from now on, my son."

Crossing his right hand across his chest, Lunitar stayed on his knee for a minute before standing to face his father. "I appreciate the honor and confidence you bestow on me, but is not Gideon firstborn here?"

Reivn frowned at the question. He recognized why there was confusion, but he disliked having to explain himself where Gideon was concerned. "Gideon will not be released from his position anytime soon. He still has much to learn about tactics and the art of warfare. His performance on the field tonight was not what it should have been."

"I understand, father, but... his performance does not change the fact he is the firstborn. Does not the lineage and mantle transfer to the eldest? I am not questioning your decision. I'm just wondering why the deviation?"

Walking over to the fireplace, Reivn knelt down and put in a few logs. Then using the Spirals, he lit them with ease. Finally, he turned around. "I have known Gideon for many years longer than you have even been alive. For personal reasons I will not divulge, I do not trust him. Were he the only child I had, I still would not make him my second. He will never have that privilege. My lands and title will pass to whomever I choose, should the need ever occur. There is also more to this family than you know, but I do not have the time to explain. It will have to wait. So just accept my decision and leave it alone."

Lunitar gazed at him in surprise. Then he bowed, realizing any objections would be pointless. "I understand. Thank you, father. I will not fail you. I may disappoint or displease you, but I will never betray you."

Reivn stood up and walked back to his desk, where he picked up a letter he had penned and sealed with his crest. Then he walked over to Lunitar and handed it to him. "This guarantees you're a free man, my heir, and a commissioned officer. If anything should happen to me, take that directly to the Council. However, do not break that seal for any reason until you are standing before them. It is fused with my magic... a signature that cannot be refuted. Keeping it intact would mean the difference between life and death for everyone here. I will be leaving tonight."

Staring at it in surprise, Lunitar replied quietly, "It will be as you command, my lord." Then he looked up in concern. "So you go to fight amongst the wars of men again? Watch your back, father. You are one of the best swordsmen I know, but even a blundering squire with a sword in the right place at the right time can bring down a master swordsman. I know what you face, and I know how limited you will be. I only ask one favor. I just got to this position. Let me fill it for a few centuries."

"I do not intend to die out there," Reivn replied quietly. "However, I do share your concerns. Fighting among humans is never the same as fighting amongst our own kind. My magic is useful, but I do agree with the Council on this. Using it among humans is too dangerous. They do not trust us as they once did." Reivn sighed and put his hand on Lunitar's shoulder. "Understand this. You are free from the tyranny of Mastric as a servant, but we are all still slaves to the Council's will. So I will go where they send me, and pray I return home when it is done."

Lunitar nodded and bowed his head. He knew how true his words were. He had lived it as Mastric's servant for many centuries.

Reivn quickly gathered what he would need. "I do not know how long I will be gone, so I left instructions with the Guard Commander. He will help you learn to run things here in my absence." Then he stopped and looked over at his son. "Do not worry. I am not that easy to kill."

When he was ready, they walked to the portal room together. Reivn gave as much information as possible about the Keep's daily operations, along with a list of who he could ask for help. Then right before he stepped through the portal, he said, "As far as Gideon goes... keep him practicing in the arena. I will retest him when I return." Then he was gone.

Lunitar stared at the portal in shock. Trying to absorb what had just happened, he stood there in stunned silence. In just a few years, he had gone from being a slave to becoming the son of a prominent Elder, and was now that Elder's second and in command of an entire fortress. He turned almost automatically and headed for the library, needing to feel some normalcy to the night. On his way, he stopped by the Commander's office.

The Commander immediately rose to his feet and saluted. Everyone knew Lunitar now, and the warning Reivn had left commanding that they obey him rang loudly in his ears. "My lord, how may I help you?"

"Tonight, I am going to the library," Lunitar replied, returning his salute. "If any emergencies arise, you can find me there. Tomorrow, I want you to show me everything to effectively and efficiently run this fortress." Then he paused before adding, "Do not hold anything back. Whenever one of us steps through that portal, there is always a chance we will not come home. So the rest of us need to know how to carry on until if or when they return." Then without waiting for an answer, he turned and left, walking at a brisk pace down the halls. It was not until he was in the library and settled into a chair that he let out a deep breath. Then he sat back and stared at the rows of books, his thoughts wandering to the nights ahead and just how hard it would be to actually wait for Reivn's return.

# THE BLOODLINE

## Chapter Seven
## Egyptian Princess

Six months went by with no word from Reivn.

Lunitar focused on continuing his studies and learning all about the fortress's operations. As each night passed without news of his father, he grew more uneasy.

Then after months of waiting, Reivn finally stumbled through the portal. He was covered in wounds, some of them rather serious... and he was not alone.

A raven-haired woman with smooth alabaster skin and dark eyes helped him down from the platform. She immediately turned to the surprised guard. "Send for a Cleric at once! Your lord needs attention!"

The guard paled and scrambled around the desk, rushing to Reivn's aid. Then seeing the depth of his injuries, he quickly telepathied Lunitar. *My lord, your father has returned wounded. He is presently being assisted by a lady, but he needs a Cleric. Please come at once.*

Lunitar looked up from his reading, a worried look crossing his features. He dropped the book and headed for the portal room at a run. *On my way!* Frustrated he had not yet mastered teleporting without a portal, he ran as fast as his skills would allow, sending a silent message to their best Cleric to join him. *You are needed in the portal chamber now! Lord Reivn is wounded!*

He met Reivn, half-carried by both the guard and the strange woman, coming down the hall. A Cleric had already joined them and was helping to ease him down to the floor.

Lunitar immediately took over. "Return to your post," he ordered the Guard. "Tell no one." Then he glanced at the woman who had brought Reivn home, wondering who she was. *Later,* he chastised himself. Turning his full attention to his father, he knelt beside him.

Reivn opened his eyes briefly and looked at his son. "The Ottomans are now a major power in Egypt and Palestine." He struggled to breathe as he spoke, making it obvious he had suffered internal injuries as well. "That is not the worst of it. Arian is dead."

Recognizing the name of the Mithranian Warlord and Commander-in-Chief of their armies, Lunitar's expression grew worried, but he pushed it aside and turned his attention to Reivn's injuries. "Rest, my lord. We will discuss these matters later. For now, we must focus on you."

The Cleric was already busy working on his more serious injuries, and after a few tense minutes of silence, found the worst of it with broken ribs and a punctured lung in his right side. One by one, she carefully moved them back in place and knitted them together with her magic before seeing

57

to healing the lung. Then she looked up. "He should be safe enough to move to his quarters now, my lord."

"Thank you," Lunitar replied. He carefully helped Reivn to his feet. "Let's get you to your rooms where you can rest comfortably."

Reivn wearily agreed. He was still very much in need of care, but he was at least standing on his own. He held out his hand to the woman. "Come," he said. Then he glanced at his son. "She stays with me for now."

The woman took his hand in silence, and then smiled at Lunitar, but when she looked at him, her eyes flashed gold for a moment before returning to their previous dark shade.

Somewhat taken aback, Lunitar was not sure he had seen right. There was only one tribe he knew of whose eyes could turn that color, and they were not part of the Alliance. As he helped his father through the halls to his quarters, he was silent, watching their guest from the corner of his eye and wondering who she was.

Reivn was relieved when they finally settled him into his bed, and he closed his eyes, allowing the Cleric to continue the healing of his injuries.

Their guest sat down on the bed next to him and began helping her. "I could have helped you sooner, you know," she said with a soft laugh. "It would have been easy for me."

"Had you done so, you would have revealed yourself to everyone, human and Vampyre alike," he admonished. "I was not going to let you risk your life that way. Not when I could cover us both."

She laughed at that. "You really are a hero. And here I thought you Mastrics were positively boring. Really, Reivn. If not for their numbers... well... let's just say I would still be in Egypt."

Gazing up at her, Reivn shook his head. "Had you tried to fight them with your magic, you would have revealed us all. That was why I intervened when I did. However, seeing as I robbed you of your home, you are welcome to stay here as long as you like."

She smiled at him. "I will take you up on that, for now at least. I certainly need time to make other arrangements. I was sad to see Arian leave us. I will feel that loss for some time, I fear..." She sighed and looked away, dabbing at her eyes.

Lunitar stood by, listening to their conversation in silence. This woman made him uncomfortable in ways he could not explain. Finally, he said, "My lord, should I contact the Quartermaster and have him arrange quarters for our guest?"

Reivn turned and looked at him. "Forgive me, Lunitar. I failed to introduce you. This is Alora Leopold. I accidently displaced her from her home in Egypt when I attacked the soldiers who had her surrounded."

"I was not surrounded. I was negotiating, but no matter. We are where we are." Alora sighed and patted Reivn's shoulder. "Your son is right. I need quarters and a bath, and you need rest."

Lunitar bowed slightly, turning to gaze at Alora. "Thank you, my lady..." he stated politely, acknowledging her. Then he looked at Reivn. "My lord, with your permission, I will continue to see to the Keep's operations until you are able to resume your duties."

With a chuckle, Reivn nodded. Then he clicked his tongue in disapproval. "You need not be so formal, Lunitar. She and I have become well-acquainted these last few weeks. Alora, please assure my son he can be at ease with you. I am afraid I upturned everything here with my rather abrupt arrival tonight."

Alora smiled and got up. Then straightening her skirts, she walked over to Lunitar and curtsied. "It is nice to meet you. Do not worry. I assure you, I will be no bother at all. I do not plan on staying long."

"As you say, my lady." Lunitar replied calmly, showing no outward emotion. He was very uneasy. Something about this woman seemed off to him. "Shall I see you to your quarters? They will be ready when we arrive." He quickly telepathied the Quartermaster to prep the rooms he had in mind, and then held out his hand to her expectantly.

With a smile, she nodded and allowed him to escort her to the door. "Thank you, lord Reivn," she stated over her shoulder. "It gives me time to plan my next move." Then she sighed and followed Lunitar from the room.

Lunitar let go of her the second they stepped into the hall. Then he led her down the corridor. He was silent as they walked, not trusting her.

However, Alora was seemingly at ease. "You do not talk much, do you?" she asked politely.

"No, my lady. I do not," he replied stiffly. "Do not think me rude, but I prefer the company of books and tomes to that of people." *and there is definitely something wrong with you...* he added silently.

Alora smiled and looked right at him. "Why would you think that?" she crooned. "Have I not been kind enough to your father?"

Taken aback that she could read his thoughts, Lunitar stopped walking and turned to stare at her. Quickly regaining his composure, he said, "I apologize for my rudeness, my lady. I am suspicious of strangers, and these last few months have been difficult ones."

"Well, your master has returned to you in one piece, so you can be at ease," she replied with a smile. "Poor Arian wasn't so lucky..." Then she sighed in frustration. "Such a waste."

Lunitar did not respond and walked the rest of the way in silence. When they reached her rooms, he left her at the door, promising to send someone for her to feed from before dawn. He was anxious to return to Reivn's side to see how his healing was coming.

Reivn was sitting up in bed and much more clear-headed than he had been when Lunitar left. He smiled at his son. "Thank you for seeing to Alora's comfort. I could not in good conscience leave her in a fallen country with nowhere to go. I have kept her beside me since we left Egypt. I intend to see her safely settled into a new haven, as I deprived her of her previous one. Hiding her during that final battle was not easy. She is quite strong-willed, that one. I look forward to getting to know her better. A test of wills is always interesting."

"Well, not to speak ill of our guest, father, but be mindful. She is telepathically intrusive," Lunitar warned him.

With a laugh, Reivn nodded and glanced up. "That she is! I am sorry. I forgot you have never met a Semerkhetian before. They have rather... interesting abilities. She is harmless enough. I gathered she does not hold to the ways of her tribe. Perhaps that was why she was alone when I found her."

Lunitar's eyes widened at the mention of her tribe. "She is a Semerkhetian and you brought her here as a guest?" he asked in shock. "I am confused."

"Yes. She is our guest," Reivn reaffirmed. "She has no ties to the Principatus. She was in no way standing against our efforts in Egypt, nor was she committing any crime or violence when I came across her. I am still getting to know her, but I feel she is simply as they say... a fish out of water." He paused and then added, "Perhaps time among us will allow her the luxury of going before the Council to claim acceptance. Then she would be free to move among us instead of remaining alone as she was."

"Very well, my lord," Lunitar replied quietly. "It will be as you command." Then he turned his attention to other matters. "Would you like the full report on Gideon now or later?"

Reivn glanced up at the mention of Gideon's name. "Now will do. How much of a problem has he been?"

Surprised by his bitter tone, Lunitar frowned. "He's been working hard in the arena and library every night since you left. Honestly, he's as skilled as I am in both sword and magic now, father. He merely lacks your guidance in our war tactics at this point, and he is not alone in that. I have not yet been tried in this war."

Silence filled the room as Reivn digested what Lunitar told him. Finally, he looked up. "I will assess his abilities myself, and we shall see whether or not I find him ready. I do not trust his honesty toward you or anyone else for that matter. He is good at deceiving others, and to be honest, I am not sure I am ready to allow him so much power."

Lunitar quickly realized this was their history talking and not Gideon's readiness for anything. It was personal for Reivn, and he knew that further pursuing it would not be wise. So, he changed the subject. "Father, if I may inquire... I knew it would be a difficult campaign, but how was it such a complete failure? I only ask because you would not have come home in this condition otherwise."

Reivn swung his legs over the side of the bed and got up, wanting to bathe and change. "The odds were always stacked against us, because we could not use our magic. However, I think one of the Warlords made a serious error in judgement, and that is what cost Arian his life." He turned to look at Lunitar, his face briefly filled with guilt. "I was not able to reach him. What I do not understand, however, is why Valfort did not try to. He could have made it in time." He paused in contemplation. "Perhaps he did not see him until it was too late..."

Lunitar could hear the doubt in his voice. "Valfort is a lot of things, but an unobservant fool... that's a tough one to swallow. However, you were there, and I was not."

Walking to the closet to retrieve fresh clothes, Reivn stopped to gaze at Lunitar in concern. "That may well be. Either way, I will not be the one who condemns him to Mastric. We both know what that would mean for him. I will let the inquiry play out among the Warlords. It is not my place to do so, and I prefer to avoid becoming a part of it."

Lunitar realized that like himself, Reivn wanted no part of the political battles the high-ranking Elders faced every night, and he half-smiled. "I understand, my lord. Will there be anything else tonight?"

Reivn shook his head, distracted by his own thoughts. "No. I believe I will bathe, and then retire to my office for the remainder of the evening. I feel rather tired tonight."

Understanding all too well, Lunitar bowed and left to return to his studies in the library. On his way, he contacted the Commander. *Post extra guards in the hall where our guest is staying, outside the library, and his Lordship's quarters as well.* He was taking no chances.

After Lunitar left, Reivn wearily headed to the baths. His thoughts were far darker than he had told his son. Arian's death was in fact a crushing blow to the Alliance, and one he could not take lightly. *How does a Mithranian of his ability lose a battle with humans. There is no finer warrior on this planet. They are masters of weaponry and warfare. What happened was to all intents and purposes impossible, and yet...* He shook himself, playing out what he had seen again, trying to make sense of it.

The birthright of the Mithranians was legendary. It made them the finest warriors and assassins in existence. So to have mere humans take one down was unheard of. He was more than a little disturbed by it. Arian had been their Commander-in-Chief since the tribal Warlords had first been created following Oberon's death. He had been one of the most powerful of the Elders, and when it came to his prowess in battle, he had no equal.

*What am I not seeing here?* Reivn wondered as he slipped into the hot water to ease the aching in his body. He leaned his head back against the edge of the bath, the warmed tiles beneath him offering comfort as he closed his eyes. He stayed there for hours, lost in his own thoughts.

When he finally got to his office, he put aside all thoughts of their defeat and dug into the paperwork piled on his desk. Distracted by both recent events and his work, he did not hear the knock on his door.

"There you are," a sultry voice said from the entryway. "May I come in?" Alora gazed at him seductively.

Reivn looked up. Then sitting back, he motioned for her to enter. From the hall, he could hear a guard reposition himself outside the door and knew Lunitar was having her watched. "Have you settled in all right? Do you need anything?" He was still somewhat distracted, but he welcomed her company, nonetheless.

She smiled and looked down at her attire. "A change of clothes perhaps... As you know I didn't have time to grab anything."

"Of course. My apologies for that oversight," he replied and got up. "Come... I'll take you to our seamstress." He opened the door for her and then caught her hand in his. "I am glad you are here. These old halls could use a little beauty in them."

Alora laughed and joined him. "You have a silver tongue, Reivn. I imagine you have a lady in every city who falls for your charms. However, I am a much harder catch. Call it... high expectations."

Reivn did not respond. He merely smiled and kept walking until they reached a small shop tucked back in a corner of one of the lower levels of the Keep. Then he opened the door for her, and they went in.

The seamstress looked up. "Oh, my lord! Welcome home! What can I do for you?"

"This lady needs some clothing suiting her station," he replied. "She is a guest here. So, I will cover any expenses necessary. Finest materials and whatever she wants. Have some of the servants aid you until she has what she needs." Then he turned to Alora. "I leave you in most capable hands. There is a guard outside who will take you back to your quarters once she has your measurements and selections. They will be ready when you wake tomorrow."

Alora glanced at the woman and smiled. "This will be fun, I think. It has been a while since I had something new from this region." Then she put her hand on his cheek and caressed it. "Careful not to spoil me too much, Reivn. I might get used to it."

Gazing down at her, he was momentarily captivated by her sultry dark eyes. "Would that really be so bad?" he asked quietly, capturing her hand as she pulled it away. Then he gently kissed her palm before letting her go and heading out.

Alora watched him until he disappeared around a corner. Then her eyes narrowed, and her thoughts grew dark. *You can try your hardest, Commander, but you are merely a pleasant distraction. I have a much higher goal in mind and unfortunately, you cannot help me achieve it.*

# THE BLOODLINE

## Chapter Eight
## First Knight

Reivn spent the next few weeks frequenting Alora's company when he was not handling Fortress affairs.

Lunitar watched from a distance, his concern over his father's affection for her growing with every passing night. Though she showed no outward signs indicating she was anything other than what she claimed, he still could not shake the feeling something was wrong.

One night, he was sitting in the library thinking about Reivn's recent infatuation and how he could secure more information about the focus of his interest when Gideon walked in and sat down beside him.

"What's wrong, Lunitar?" Gideon put his books on the table and crossed his arms, gazing intently at his brother. "I know that look. Something is bothering you."

Heaving a sigh, Lunitar looked at his brother. "I am concerned over father's infatuation with Alora. I have known him for over twelve hundred years, and I've never seen him show this much interest in a woman before. It's uncharacteristic for him."

Gideon grinned and scratched his chin. "Perhaps he just needed the right one to come along for that to happen. I heard he was married once before, and that she was a particularly magnificent woman." He paused and pulled a book over in front of him. Then he began perusing its pages, not daring to look up. "Some men are very particular in their tastes. From what I gather, she doesn't show anything other than a casual interest in return. So, I doubt anything will come of it either way."

"I had not heard that rumor. However, I know you and father have a history that spans beyond my knowledge, so perhaps you know something of him I don't." Lunitar replied with a frown. "I'm just concerned because..." He paused and sighed. "If I tell you something, you have to promise never to say anything to father about it. I know there is tension between you, and I think this would only exacerbate the problem in your relationship."

Gideon stared at him, somewhat taken aback by his candor. "That is a pretty big build up, brother. But yes, I can swear to never say anything. To be honest, I hardly ever see father anyway. He tends to avoid me. I haven't even met Alora yet."

Lunitar glanced at the door to be sure they were alone. Then he said, "She is a Semerkhetian... one of the two Principatus tribes and our sworn enemy."

"She's what?" Gideon's jaw dropped in shock. "Does father know?"

With a nod, Lunitar closed the book in front of him, having lost interest in reading. "He was the one who made me aware of this," he answered quietly.

Gideon could not believe what he was hearing. "If he knows, then why would he... I mean, he brought her here and is treating her like royalty."

"I see that as well," Lunitar replied with a frown. "I do not know the specifics on how they met, and frankly, I am not going to ask. However, do not think for a second that I believe the dribble coming from her mouth. If she so much as makes the slightest of threats toward him, I will use any means necessary to utterly destroy her."

Closing his own book, Gideon pushed it aside. "Count me in," he agreed wholeheartedly. "I'm still trying to prove to him that I am not the same person I was all those years ago. I will do whatever it takes to protect him from her or anyone else who threatens him."

"Then we will sit back and observe for now, sharing what we know." Lunitar was somewhat relieved Gideon wanted to help him, but before he could say anything, he received a summons.

*Lunitar, report to my office at once.* Reivn's tone was urgent.

"Father has just requested my presence," he told Gideon. "We will talk more later." Then he got up and hurried out the door.

Reivn was pacing his office when Lunitar arrived. "Good. You are here. We need to talk. I have been summoned to Mastric's halls. I leave tonight."

Concern crossing his features, Lunitar frowned. "My lord... did Mastric find out about our guest?"

"I honestly do not know," Reivn admitted, his expression worried. "I am hoping this is more about Arian's death than anything to do with Alora. I am planning to take her to the Council to seek asylum, but I am not prepared to do that just yet. I need more time."

Lunitar stared at him, shocked by his declaration. "Very well, father. I will see to the Keep and our guest's needs until your return."

Reivn nodded and handed him the necessary paperwork. "Please let Gideon know I will see him when I return. I have not spoken to him much these last few weeks. I have been rather busy." He held back from saying more, feeling guilty.

Knowing the true reason for his neglect, Lunitar said nothing.

Then Reivn cleared his throat uncomfortably at the awkward silence. "Yes, well... I have to make my final preparations. I will return as soon as I am able. You are in command."

Lunitar bowed. "Then I will take my leave, my lord."

Reivn nodded and followed him out, locking the door behind him. Then they went their separate ways as he headed for the portal chamber and London.

Three nights went by with no word and Lunitar began to worry. The state of affairs in the Alliance had been uncertain since Arian's death, and there were still no updates as to the new appointment of a Commander-in-Chief in his place. Such chaos threatened the stability of their entire society. He kept constant watch over Alora, but she rarely ventured from her rooms, preferring to lounge in the silence alone.

Gideon spent as much of his time in the library or arena as possible, frequently working himself so hard he needed the care of a Cleric in the early hours before dawn.

Finally, on the fourth night, Reivn stepped through the portal, weary, but otherwise unharmed. Not bothering to go to his chambers, he immediately telepathied Lunitar. *Where are you?*

Lunitar's response was instantaneous. *In the Commonroom.*

Too exhausted to walk, Reivn teleported instead, and found Lunitar sitting with a few tomes on the sofa in front of the fire.

Looking up from his books when Reivn appeared, Lunitar immediately realized something was wrong. "What is the matter, father?"

Reivn sat down across from him, leaned back, and closed his eyes. "Arian's death has had a huge impact on the Alliance."

Lunitar closed his book and set it on the table in front of him. Then he walked over to the bar and grabbed two glasses and a bottle of blood-laced rum. He carried them over to where his father was seated and set them on the table. Then he poured them both a drink and sat back down.

"My father convened all the Elders in London and demanded answers of us all. The Council is in an uproar and Mithras wants accountability." Reivn paused, picked up the rum, and downed it quickly. "It would seem that my fool of a brother made yet another mistake... and this time, it has brought the war to our doorstep."

Sitting forward, Lunitar stared at his father in shock. "Am I to understand that Valfort's error directly contributed to Arian's death?"

Reivn rubbed his forehead trying to ease the fatigue he felt. "Yes, but it does not stop there. Out of necessity, the Council must appoint another Commander-in-Chief. The problem is my father wants me to go with him to the Council's chambers. He has chosen me as an elect for the position."

"Question, father. Not that I doubt your ability, but isn't the Warlord usually considered for these positions?" Lunitar asked in confusion.

"You are correct. As to why my father selected me instead of my brother, I have no answer for that. However, I suspect it is because his mistakes are too frequent to be considered for such a responsibility. He has only remained our Warlord because Mastric does not have anyone he considers a suitable candidate to replace him." Reivn paused and turned to look at him. "I dare not disobey my father's summons. If chosen, however, this will only further sour Valfort against me. It is a position I do not want, nor have ever coveted. Being their Commander-in-Chief also means I will never be free to live the life I desire."

Lunitar shook his head in disbelief. "That's an understatement, but I believe there is more to it politically. You said Mithras wants accountability and Valfort..." He paused. "Valfort is the obvious choice because he's not even the scapegoat here. If he's responsible for Arian's death, Mastric will offer him up as a sacrificial lamb." He sat back, somewhat shaken by the thought. "My best guess is that Valfort will be stripped of his title at best. At worst, he will be executed. We both know how much Mastric dislikes being made a fool of."

Reivn stared at Lunitar, realizing he was right. This could be far more than just a bid for a Mastrics Commander-in-Chief. "If Mastric wants me to take the oath, then I will have no choice but to comply."

His words carried much weight, and Lunitar could hear the burden he felt so heavily in his voice. "You and I both know this will push our family to the forefront... not only under the scrutiny of Mastric, but the Council and all the tribes as well."

Closing his eyes again, Reivn leaned back, the emotions he felt at the idea of so many lives resting on his shoulders overwhelming him. "God help us all in the nights ahead..." he whispered.

Lunitar stared at the fire, lost in his own thoughts. Finally, he asked simply, "When do you leave?"

"Tomorrow night..."

The following night, Lunitar and Gideon both stood in the portal chamber with Reivn.

Reivn handed a sealed letter to Lunitar. "Hold onto this. If they select me, then you will need to open it. It transfers leadership of the Honor Guard to you in the event of my change of rank and station, and promotes you to the rank of Commander in my place."

Lunitar raised an eyebrow and gazed at the letter in his hand in surprise. "Yes, my lord..." he said with no small amount of doubt.

"I did not pick you because of who you are," Reivn stated, putting his hand on Lunitar's shoulder to reassure him. "You are quite capable of the task. I trained you well." Then he turned to Gideon. "I will say this only once. I have noticed how hard you train, and I have seen your sincerity. We will sit down and talk when I return. There are things I want to tell you, and answers I need to hear. Until then, help your brother and learn the Keep's operations. We have busy nights ahead."

Gideon's eyes filled with hope and he straightened up, standing proudly in front of him. "Yes, father! Thank you! I won't disappoint you!"

Reivn turned and prepared to open the portal when a voice called out from the hallway.

"Reivn! I heard you were back! You are leaving again already?" Alora hurried into the room, her lips pursed into a pout. "I have been so bored of late. Can you not stay a little longer?"

With a sigh, he walked over and took her hand, kissing her cheek gently. "I am sorry. Duty calls. My father has summoned me. However, if all goes well, I will not have to wait any longer to ask for your asylum." Then he glanced past her to Lunitar. "Take good care of her in my absence. I cannot have her getting upset for lack of company. Perhaps it would be a good time for you to get to know her."

Lunitar bowed slightly in acknowledgement. "Perhaps, father. I will ensure she wants for nothing in your absence."

Alora smoothed back a stray lock of hair, and then brazenly put her arms around his neck. "Well... I miss you already," she pouted again and kissed him on the lips.

Stunned, Reivn slowly wrapped his arms around her and pulled her into his embrace, kissing her properly. Then when he let her go and saw the expressions on his son's faces, he cleared his throat in embarrassment. "I had... best be off. Mastric will not be pleased if I am late."

Lunitar and Gideon waited until he had gone. Then Lunitar turned to Alora. "My lady, is there anything you need that I can help with?" he asked her politely.

Alora laughed and patted his cheek. "Not at all. I am quite content right now. We do have many busy nights ahead, after all." Then she strolled out into the hall and looped her arm through the arm of the Guard who was waiting for her. "I am off to my rooms so you can talk about me uninterrupted. Good night."

"As you wish, my lady," Lunitar answered calmly, watching her go. He was not going to let her draw him into a confrontation.

However, Gideon tightened his fist and took a step forward, prepared to argue with her.

Lunitar put his hand on Gideon's chest, stopping him. Then he turned to look at him and asked, "Will you join me in the Commonroom?"

Indignant by her accusation, Gideon opened his mouth to challenge it, but as he caught Lunitar's expression, he closed it again and nodded. His eyes flashed with anger, but he understood.

The two of them walked down the hall together in silence until they were well out of Alora's earshot.

However, Gideon could not stand the silence any longer and blurted out, "Why did you stop me? I would have set her straight! She kissed him! And he kissed her back!"

"I'm well aware of what we both saw. You would have fallen right into her trap," Lunitar glanced at him, understanding his outrage, as his own feelings were not far from it as well. "That whole display was for us. Didn't you see how surprised father was?"

With a growl, Gideon nodded. "I did, but then he kissed her back! What was that if not acceptance?"

Lunitar shook his head. "Again... a display on her part to elicit a response from us, and it appears to have worked on you."

"Maybe so, but now she has free run of the fortress, and we have been ordered to entertain her and keep her happy!" Gideon was furious.

"No. We were ordered to take care of her, not to cater to her. We interpret how we take care of her," Lunitar reminded him.

Gideon was silent for a minute as he thought about it. "Then does this mean we're going to keep her in her rooms?"

"Not entirely," Lunitar replied, thinking hard as he tried to figure out a way around their situation. "We will enact our normal military protocol. Guards are already posted outside her quarters and the library. Now, they are also going to be posted outside the armory and all other strategic facilities. I don't care if she goes to the observatory or the Commonroom. It would be even better if she decided to explore the countryside for nights on end."

With a laugh, Gideon gave him a slight shove. "You sly bastard! You are working on a way to get her to leave, aren't you?"

"Gideon, my brother, you are a skilled swordsman and you are skilled with the Spirals. Now it is time that you better learn the subtle manipulations of politics and people." They entered the Commonroom as he spoke. "Now the true political machinations are going to start. Father is going before the Council in a bid for the rank of Commander-in-Chief against eight Warlords. That will most probably be like two small children arguing over who stole who's string. The only difference is that someone could die."

Gideon fell silent, suddenly seeing their situation in a whole new light. "Dear God... if they select father, he will not sit in the back and give orders. He will take the lead and be out in front... He isn't the kind of man to order others where he is not willing to go. If I know nothing else about him, I know he will die before letting another man fall at his behest. He's going to need us now more than ever..."

Lunitar sobered at the thought and turned to look at him. "Then we must train with renewed earnest and prepare for the long nights ahead."

"Please teach me everything you know, Lunitar... I must be ready to stand with him also," Gideon begged, his eyes reflecting his desire. "You have his respect, and you have his love. Show me how to be like him. I see so much, and yet still feel like I continue to fall short of what I should be. Teach me what honor is as he sees it. I am his son, so the best way I can thank and honor him is to be as he would have me be."

Surprised by his passionate outburst, Lunitar put his hand on Gideon's shoulder, stopping his tirade. "You are my brother, and always will be. You never have to beg for me to teach you anything. Just tell me what you want to know and if it is in my power to teach you, then I will."

Gideon reached up and gripped his hand, squeezing it gratefully before pulling away. "Then please tell me what honor is to him and how he sees the world? I want to understand him, but above all, I want to show him I have changed and become the man he wanted me to be."

"To answer the question on how father views honor would take me centuries to explain to you. Continue as you have been and watch others, and you will learn. Always uphold integrity and justice, and defend the innocent and downtrodden. Father has noticed your change. He has noticed your dedication. Do not try to be him. Be yourself with his ideals. Father and I are very similar, but we have our differences as well. You just haven't been around long enough yet to see them. Also, understand father is not one to show a lot of emotional affection. That has never been a problem for me because frankly, I have none. However, I see... no... I have forgotten how important it is to others. Father initially kept you around and trained you out of a sense of duty, but that is changing. There is fondness there. I see it. So keep doing what you are doing, and you will achieve your goal."

Gideon dropped his gaze and stared at the floor. "I hope you are right," he whispered. Then he looked up. "Can we still train together?"

"That has never been a question. Yes," Lunitar smiled and pulled a book down from one of the shelves that lined the walls. Then he held it up and showed it to Gideon. It was a tome on the practical uses of combat magic. "How about we start with this?"

# THE BLOODLINE

## Chapter Nine
## Fallen Elder

Elena was waiting for Reivn when he arrived at the London Guild. "Father is expecting you in the South wing, in your old laboratory."

"Why is he in my lab and not his own?" Reivn felt a knot growing in his stomach, but he remained expressionless, not wanting to give any indication he was worried.

She took his arm and walked with him. "Come, brother. You know that does not work with me. You are in no trouble. The same cannot be said for Ceros though. He has angered father this time, I fear, far more than he can readily undo."

He sighed and shook his head. "If father chooses to merely punish Valfort for this one, he should consider himself lucky. His repeated rebellion is a common discussion among the Warlords these days, and the loss of Arian is by far, the worst outcome that has ever occurred because of his lone wolf nonsense."

"Well, there are definitely changes in the wind," she told him, giving his hand a gentle squeeze. "Mastric is wasting no time trying to clean up the mess Ceros has made of this. He does not like the Council looking at us so hard." Then she leaned in closer and whispered, "You should know Seth is still alive. Father is training him."

Distracted by her sudden revelation, Reivn faltered in his steps for a moment and stopped to stare at her. "I dared not hope..." he whispered, and then quickly looked around to be sure they were still alone. "Please tell Seth I want him to be obedient to Mastric and serve him well."

Elena glanced up in surprise. "I can try, but it may not be so easy as you think. Even I have not been allowed to see him since he tried to leave. Mastric has him locked away."

Realizing he could get her into trouble, he simply nodded. "Then leave it alone for now."

They cut their conversation short as they arrived at his old lab, and she squeezed his hand before hurrying away.

The door opened before he even raised his hand to knock. "Come in, Reivn. We have much to discuss, and we leave in an hour."

Reivn cautiously stepped inside and sat down as the door closed behind him. "My lord?" he ventured tentatively.

Mastric shifted slightly as he raised his hand and lowered his hood. Where his face should have been was only vacant space. Then ignoring his son's shocked expression, he got up. "Your brother is in disgrace. He is no longer fit to be a Warlord. I would replace him with Shaadrakh, but that is impossible because he left us. So... I am appointing you as Warlord to the

Mastric's tribe, effective immediately, since we are leaving for the Council's deliberations concerning your appointment as Commander-in-Chief."

Stunned not only by his father's appearance, but by his revelations, Reivn was speechless. *My brother left us... Does this mean he is dead?*

"What you see before you is my consciousness. What was once my body is now one with the Spirals. Only three others have been allowed the privilege of this knowledge, so you will keep it to yourself." Mastric rose from his seat and floated around the table to hover in front of Reivn. "Shaadrakh's fate is not your concern. Get up," he ordered.

Reivn slowly got to his feet, wondering what else he would learn before the night's end. "My lord, I am your servant," he replied humbly and bowed his head. "I will, of course, accept any task you assign me."

Mastric replaced his hood and stared down at his son. "You are stronger than most of your brethren. Only Elena and Valfort have your strength, and Elena is a healer, not a warrior as you and Valfort are. So that leaves you alone able to fill the position Valfort so blatantly squandered. The other tribes will see us as weak if you cannot succeed in this, and that... I will not allow." Within seconds he had manifested his physical form. Then he held up his wrist for Reivn to feed. "You will need this tonight."

Without hesitation, Reivn knelt in front of him and drank. Raw power flooded through him, burning like liquid fire as it coursed through his veins. Visibly shaken from the powerful influx of magic, Reivn slowly got to his feet, and then bowed. "I will not fail you, my lord."

Giving him only a moment to recover, Mastric took his arm. "Come. It is time. The Council awaits our presence. As far as you are concerned, however, you do not yet know the position is yours. Leave that to me."

Polusporta Castle was bustling with activity when Mastric and Reivn arrived. Mastric had chosen to teleport them both directly into the throne room, and when they emerged from the thick black mist, it was to a crowded grand hall. The nine thrones, set in a semi-circle, were almost all occupied, the Council of Ancients having convened when news of Arian's death had spread. The other Warlords had already joined them and were discussing the events surrounding the tragedy. However, when Reivn appeared beside Mastric, all eyes shifted their way, and the room fell deathly quiet.

Arian's sire, the Ancient named Mithras, eyed Reivn coldly. "Isn't this your youngest son? Where is your Warlord?"

"Reivn is our Warlord," Mastric announced. "I stripped the title from Valfort and remanded him to severe punishment for his negligence."

With a snarl, Mithras rose from his throne. "Negligence? What negligence? He deliberately ignored Arian's call for help! He allowed my son to die!"

Mastric floated across the room to his throne and settled in, before turning to gaze at his brother. "That is why he is no longer a Warlord. I have promoted Reivn because he is not only more loyal to this Council, but also because he is more efficient. He will be ten times the leader Valfort ever was. This is why I also recommend him as our next Commander-in-Chief."

The Thylacinian Warlord, Lucian, spoke up then. "I have seen him in battle, my lord. He is skillful with both his magic and a blade. I have also heard about his moral code. Most of us here have. He is both fair and honorable. There are some among us that are either not respected enough to be able to lead or are not prepared to do so. As a Thylacinian, I know few would follow me, but they would perhaps, follow him."

"And what about retribution?" Mithras spat angrily. "My son is dead! You bring this whelp here and offer him forward, and you think it will right the wrong done to my tribe?"

Hissing like a snake, Mastric leaned forward, both his glyph and the power in his eyes flaring to a brilliant blue glow. "The wrongdoing was Valfort's, and he will pay for his failure dearly. However, it is no fault of either mine or Reivn's. He is here because he holds more knowledge of battle tactics and strategies than any other Warlord present, and he has the leadership qualities we are looking for."

Victus, who was both their King and the progenitor of the Victulian line, sat forward on his throne, listening with interest. "So, this is the candidate you told me about, Mastric. I have heard much concerning his exploits. He is indeed an accomplished warrior, but is he prepared to take on the mantle of leadership for the entire Alliance army?"

Mastric gazed expectantly at Reivn, and his telepathy cut through the young Warlord's mind with ease. *You must answer him yourself. Speak to them as a leader would.*

Reivn immediately stepped forward and looked around at those present. "I do not believe any of us are ever truly ready for the burdens of leadership. However, I am prepared to do whatever is necessary to lead our people to victory and defend the territories from our enemies. I have been in many battles against the Principatus, and the armies of humanity as well. I have seen comrades fall and intimately understand the meaning of loss. So, if selected as your Commander-in-Chief, I will uphold the laws and tenets, and will serve you to the utmost of my abilities."

A young woman near Mithras dropped to one knee before Mithras. "My lord. I know you selected me as the new Warlord for the Mithranians, fully expecting me to request the mantle of leadership tonight. However, I believe I could better serve you in other ways. As Warlord, my duties are to my tribe, and I am prepared to execute those, but I do not believe I have the experience Lord Reivn does. So I respectfully request my name is withdrawn from the bid for leadership."

Mithras gazed down at her fondly, before resuming his seat. "Get up, Leshye. You humble yourself too much. You are a skilled warrior in your own right and every bit an equal to this Mastric. Arian was one of us, and he held the mantle of leadership from the time our armies were formed until his death. Why should leadership be given to any other tribe now?"

From the floor in front of one of the thrones, a low growl rose. Thylacinos stretched and got up, sauntering over to Reivn to inspect him closer. "You believe he is a better choice than mine, Mastric. Leshye seems to agree with you and does not want the position either, but what of the rest of the warlords? Are they willing to follow him? A warrior he may be, but he has never led any of them into battle before."

Seated next to Victus, a woman of ethereal beauty stirred in her seat, brushing a wisp of golden blond hair from her eyes. Her soft voice filled the room. "It is interesting that a Mastric caused the downfall of the Commander-in-Chief, and now the Mastrics want to place one of their own in that role. Poor Arian..." The suggestion she made, though unspoken, was obvious. She was accusing Mastric of having planned Arian's sudden demise.

Mastric growled and turned his icy gaze on her. "You dare, Galatia? I might learn to watch who you accuse of betrayal if I were you. Those are very dangerous words. It is well-known by everyone present that Valfort has a history of disobedience, and a fondness of doing as he pleases. He has been repeatedly punished, at times severely. It did not mend his ways. So I have removed him from doing any further harm. Now if he continues to be disobedient, he will forfeit his life. As far as this Council is concerned, I merely seek to repair the damage done by offering up my youngest and most skilled son to serve the Council as they see fit. I have dealt with Valfort's treachery, and his punishment is by far more brutal than anything he has ever before experienced. Of that, you can be sure."

Galatia closed her eyes and let out a sigh. "Something tells me this Council's meeting was once again merely a formality. Fine. I yield. Annie is not exactly leadership material in that capacity anyway. She prefers a more... intimate approach in dealing with Alliance matters, and few Galatians would want the job either way."

To her right, a Bedouin man with kind eyes, weathered tan skin and wizened features spoke up. "I would offer my own son as a candidate, but Lazar has already expressed his desire to decline. I respect that choice and will not force him to put in his name as a candidate. So we Sargonians withdraw from the candidacy. I do think Reivn is a fine choice, but I will abide by the Council's decision."

Victus gazed at his brother in approval. *This will make it easier to install him as I promised. Mastric had best deliver on his end of this.* "My son, Darius, is likewise withdrawn from the candidacy. He is a strong leader, as most Victulians are, but he lacks the skills as a warrior that would be crucial to this position."

Thylacinos turned to stare at Victus in contempt. "Are we to just hand him the appointment without a challenge then?" he snapped. "There must be a challenge. That is the law."

A woman seated to the right of Mastric got up and walked over to stare in Reivn's face, appearing to inspect him. "I had thought to stay out of this tonight, but it appears you will not allow me to do so," Armenia stated in frustration. "We Armenians have never vied for positions of power, because our interest lies in cataloging history, not making it." She turned to glare at Victus, obviously annoyed. "However, Marcus will be offering a challenge to Reivn for the position of Commander-in-Chief. There is no other way. I will not agree to this appointment unless this child proves himself."

"As will Djordji," a man at the end of the row of thrones added. Silvanus was growing impatient with all of them, and in his estimation, his son would be far more suitable than just handing the lead to a newcomer. "We Dracanas have little objections to the decisions made here in chambers, but I must agree with Armenia on this one. Reivn has never been tested as a leader, and you wish to drop him into not only the position of a Warlord, but as the Commander of our entire army. Are we forgetting what is at stake here?"

Reivn bowed his head and stared at the floor. He was not comfortable standing there on display while the Ancients argued over his head. Now he knew he would be fighting with fellow Warlords to prove his worth. He also knew Mastric would tolerate nothing less than his winning.

Mastric shrewdly recognized the unwillingness of his son to step into such a grand role and telepathied him again. *You will win this position before the night is through, or you will be buried beneath the Guild in a crypt for the next millenia for failing me. Is that understood?*

Lifting his head, Reivn met his gaze, his eyes registering understanding. The choice was not his to make. *Yes, my lord,* he quietly responded.

Mithras stared at Reivn. He knew the reputation the young Warlord had already earned. And if he truly admitted it to himself, putting Leshye in that role would risk her exposure and put her in danger, and that was something he was not prepared to do. But he was still unwilling to yield the position to Mastric's brood so easily. "Leshye shall also fight in the challenge... to test him and stand for Arian's honor. If he can best her, I will yield with no further argument."

Thylacinos grinned. "My son, Lucian, will also be fighting in the challenge," he quipped, glancing meaningfully at Lucian as he spoke. "Let us see what this Mastric is made of."

Mithras glanced at the brother seated to his left, seeking his voice.

Chronos had remained silent, listening to the argument with great restraint. He recognized that this was a power struggle by the Ancients and their children were merely pawns in it. He was not going to allow his son to become a part of that. "Alderion will withdraw from the candidacy. We Epochians have no desires on such a position. He is content enough as our Warlord. So we yield."

Pleased by their decision, Mastric looked around at them. "Then it is decided. Prepare the courtyard and let the challenge commence."

## Chapter Ten
## Rival Gods

Within the hour, the courtyard was fully lit by torches and ready for the battle to commence. Word had spread like wildfire, and a large crowd was quickly gathering.

Reivn stood watching the spectator's numbers grow, and for once was thankful none of his own were among them. After a few minutes, he closed his eyes and began mentally preparing himself for the challenge ahead. He was under no illusions about how difficult it would be. Then the sound of footsteps coming toward him made him open them again and turn around.

"I apologize for disturbing you," Leshye stated. "I just wanted to let you know this fight is not my personal choice, but it is my father's, and I must honor it. So, I will show no mercy on the battlefield."

Nodding in understanding, Reivn gazed at her intently. She was young, but her eyes held keen intelligence in them. "Nor should you," he replied. "You are a woman of honor and a warrior like me. I would never expect you to diminish yourself, regardless of the circumstances."

She half-smiled. "I was only appointed to Warlord status yesterday. How long have you..." she tapered off, not finishing her question.

"I was appointed tonight. However, I suspected it was coming. My brother makes no secret of his rebellion. However, I had hoped it would go to another of us, and not to me." Reivn looked past her to Lucian, who was standing and talking quietly with Annie and Lazar. "Watch yourself out there tonight. Our opponents will be older and stronger, and will no doubt have more power."

Leshye smiled then. "You must know how much we Mithranians train, sir, surely. I may be somewhat young in status, but I have been training and fighting for a great many years, both with my father, and with Arian when he was alive."

Reivn looked down, a twinge of guilt passing through him at the mention of Arian's name. He still wondered if he could have made a difference had he been able to reach him in time. "He was a good man, and a magnificent warrior. He will be missed in battle."

"So would you, were you to fall," Leshye stated bluntly. "His fate was also his destiny, as is yours. Each of us has a part to play, and none can know what our fate is until it arrives."

Lucian walked over and joined them. "Do either of you know how this works? You are the newcomers here, so I am assuming not."

"We are supposed to fight against each other, are we not?" Reivn asked, somewhat confused.

Lucian shook his head. "No. We are competing against each other, yes... each with our own team. However, we are to lead our teams into battle against the daemons Mastric will conjure. This fight is very real and very dangerous, and people do die. I was hoping to sit this one out, as I remember the losses the first one cost us."

Reivn frowned. "There's been one of these before?"

"Yes... when Arian became the Commander-in-Chief. It was one of the worst catastrophes the Council ever unleashed. I seriously hoped they would avoid doing this tonight and just select someone. Alderion almost died in the last one, but they do not see our worth and do not care." He paused and looked around, relieved the Ancients had not yet appeared. "Anyway, you will be getting your team shortly."

Leshye looked worried. "How do they set up the teams?" Are they all people from your own tribe or a mix? And how many?"

Lucian shrugged. "I don't know how many, but I do know it will be a mix. They want to simulate who you would lead into battle if selected. The difficult part is that we will not know what mix our teams are until we get them. It was random last time."

Reivn was staring at the arena deep in thought, only half-listening to Lucian. *Mastric conjures daemons...* It did not sit well with him. He turned to Lucian, prepared to ask another question, but the arrival of the Ancients prevented any further conversation. "Good luck," he quickly told them.

"You as well," Lucian replied and walked away.

Leshye glanced over her shoulder as she left him to join her father. "See you in battle," she smiled.

Mastric appeared beside Reivn. "Your team is a good mix, the best of the available warriors here. I saw to that. You will do well tonight. Some of the other teams... let's just say they may not fare well."

Feeling somewhat nauseous, Reivn did not answer. Instead, he focused on the groups of warriors that were entering the arena, trying to prepare himself for the coming fight. His mind was reeling at Mastric's declaration.

A team approached, and Mastric went to greet them.

Reivn quickly counted heads. *Ten warriors to how many daemons I wonder...* He walked over to join them, wanting to assess what he had in tribes and skills among them.

The other teams had joined their Warlords and were preparing for battle.

Then Mastric telepathied Reivn with last minute instructions. *Take your team to the end of the field and prepare. You have five minutes before this begins.*

Stunned at how little time they were being given, Reivn quickly turned to his team. "Follow me! We need to move now!" Then he headed for the end of the battlefield, making sure they were with him.

The other teams were moving as well, taking positions around the length of the field.

Reivn looked at the men and women beside him. "I am going to ask a single question and need only a one word answer... Your tribe?"

Each of his team members quickly responded. The answers varied... two Mithranians, three Thylacinians, an Epochian, one Sargonian, one Dracanas, and two Mastrics.

Reivn quickly assessed how he was deploying them and moved them into position. He put the three Thylacinians in the forefront and the Mithranians and Epochian behind them in a modified wedge, flattening the front line into two rows to prevent any one of them being singled out and slaughtered. Then he put the Sargonian and Dracanas in support behind them, and the Mastrics in the rear, where their magic would do the most good. Finally, he took position in the middle, so he could immediately lend support in any direction, minimizing possible losses. "Stick to weapons," he ordered. "We will be using controlled fallback tactics to draw them into a horseshoe so we can surround them and pick them off! So minimize your use of magic until I order it! Follow my lead!"

Mastric moved to the center of the courtyard and began the summoning, weaving powerful and dark magic from Tartarus itself as he opened the doorway to bring their opponents through.

And through they came... dozens of them. And though many were lesser daemons from the middle plains of Hell, several daemon warriors from the higher ranks of Tartarus also appeared.

Lucian's team had formed an inverted wedge formation and then shifted it into an almost straight line, following Reivn's example, but Marcus and Leshye's teams were still struggling to get organized.

Djordji's team had followed Reivn's example and moved to the opposite side of the field to buy themselves more time. Now they were rushing to get into a similar dual-line battle formation.

The daemons wasted no time scattering across the courtyard in clusters and charging every team present. Shrieks of delight went up as they brandished wicked claws, barbs, and razor-sharp teeth. However, the daemon warriors hung back, observing their prey and searching for the weakest points to attack before launching their own assault. Then powerful streaks of black energy began to shoot through the air. Marcus's team was their first target.

Marcus ordered shields up just in time to avoid any direct hits, but it scattered his team, and they had to scramble to regroup and defend themselves. It was every man for himself as they faced off with their attackers and recovered formation.

Chaos ruled the center of the courtyard. The daemons were in a frenzy for killing and were rapidly spreading in every direction. They had already reached Marcus and Leshye's teams. In the first moments of confusion, a few of them had caught the leg of one luckless soldier on Leshye's team and dragged him away before any of his comrades could help him. Then he was set upon and ripped to pieces. Now her team was fully engaged and fighting to defend themselves. Furious they had been caught off-guard so easily, she wielded her two katanas with incredible skill and blinding speed, her unusual fighting style helping them hold their ground.

Lucian's team was under attack by a large number of the daemons and their front men were taking a beating. They immediately began to fully invert their wedge formation, seeking a way to even the odds.

On the other side of the arena, Djordji's team was also in trouble. Not only had a large number charged them, but they had caught the notice of two of the daemon warriors as well. Now they were fighting both the physical attacks and the continued barrage of magic from above. Djordji yelled out orders as they fought to defend themselves, but within minutes, two of them were taken down and ripped apart.

A large group charged Reivn's team and they braced themselves. Determined to keep them focused, he yelled, "Wait until they're on us and fall back only when I tell you! Hold... hold..."

The first daemons reached them, and the Thylacinians in front were immediately heavily engaged. The Mithranians and Epochian joined them to hold their line, waiting for Reivn's next command.

Reivn's eyes narrowed and he yelled as another cluster of daemons reached them. "Begin to fall back!"

The Thylacinians, Mithranians and Epochian immediately began to yield ground, seemingly retreating as they moved into the U-shape formation Reivn wanted. Their movement thinned their attackers' immediate numbers, and the Mithranians and Epochian were able to slowly cut them down, while their Thylacinian comrades continued to defend the outer edges of the line.

Reivn and the Sargonian and Dracanas joined them in the thick of it. Reivn had noted all three Thylacinians were injured and that if he did not equalize their chances, he would lose good men. *This is sheer madness,* he thought. Then getting a second of reprieve, he briefly looked around, worried about the other teams.

Lucian's was holding. They had killed several daemons but were still fighting a large number of the creatures and had already lost a man.

Marcus's was in trouble. Several of their warriors had died, but the rest had managed to regroup. However, they had been pushed into a back-to-back position and were now besieged and fighting to stay alive.

Leshye's team had suffered several losses as well, but their line was holding. Her fury had shifted into frenzied determination, and she was keeping her team together as they fended off their attackers.

Then screams from across the courtyard drew Reivn's attention. Two of the daemon warriors had swooped in and grabbed Djordji, carrying him with them as they ascended. His team did everything they could to free him, but their actions were in vain. In mere seconds they had torn his body in half and dropped what was left down to the horde below, causing a feeding frenzy.

"No!" Reivn yelled. "This is insanity!" He looked around again at how quickly all the teams were losing ground. Then in sudden fury, he raised his voice, imbuing it with the power of the Spirals so it would echo throughout the courtyard. "All Warlords... all warriors... to me! One team! We do this together!"

Lucian, Leshye and Marcus all heard him and quickly assessed their situations. One by one, the decision was made. "Rally to Reivn's side! Go! Go! Fight your way through!" Lucian's team merged with Marcus's as they inched their way forward. Then Leshye's team joined them. The remains of Djordji's team struggled to move toward him as well, but they were pinned down.

Reivn turned to his own soldiers, who were still holding their line. "Push forward! We must get to the others! The only way we all survive this is to join forces! Move!" He moved to the front of his group. "Mastrics! Use the Spirals!" His voice thundered across the courtyard. Then he summoned his magic and began to unleash it on the horde.

Every Mastric responded. Lightning and fire began pouring forth, lighting up the courtyard in brilliant hues of red, blue and white. Lightning bolts struck the daemon warriors above repeatedly, burning through their wings and thick hides, and firewalls and shields went up to defend teammates as they fought their way across the field.

"Sargonians, summon your wraiths! Mithranians! Thylacinians! Shields up! Cover the Sargonians! We must get to Djordji's team!"

Reivn's orders were clear and concise, and every team responded. While their companions defended them, every Sargonian dropped to a knee, one by one closing their eyes to summon the wraiths of the aether to come forth. From the shadows, the ground, and even the air itself, wraiths emerged, rising as incorporeal figures to manifest on the field until they appeared as a small army, prepared to defend their allies from their foes.

The lesser daemons, whose minds were disorganized and easily fooled, focused their attention on these new enemies and attacked.

The wraiths fought back, brandishing spirit weapons from the shadow realm, but their bodies were not truly of flesh and blood, and their strength would not last. In an effort to reinforce them, each Sargonian poured what power they had into holding onto those summoned, anchoring their presences to the battlefield, and the connections between them and their wraiths were apparent in the threads of fine black shadows that channeled from their fingertips into those they controlled.

Once Reivn saw they were following his orders, he turned to the Epochian next to him. "I know what your birthright is, but not how strong you are. Can you slow time on multiple individuals?"

The Epochian nodded, uncertainty in his voice. "Not on our warriors surely..." he responded.

Reivn turned and pointed at the daemon warriors. "Can you slow them down?" he asked.

"I don't know! I've never tried it on a daemon before!" the Epochian answered, shaking his head.

A daemon broke through the line and ran at them, and Reivn hit him with a massive bolt of lightning, blowing him backward and into the sea of fighting figures. Then he turned to the Epochian again. "Well, there is no time like the present to find out!"

His eyes wide with fear, the Epochian nodded and turned his attention to the daemons flying above them and darting in and out among the fighting warriors on the field. Almost immediately, his eyes began to bleed liquid silver that turned into a fine mist when it hit the air and floated skyward until it settled on the flying beasts.

Reivn moved in front of him, ready to defend him from anything that tried to reach him.

The sound of battle was deafening. Lucian, Leshye and Marcus had almost reached Reivn's team, with what team members they had left, but the field behind them was littered with the bodies of their losses.

Then above them, the daemon warriors suddenly slowed, their movements becoming sluggish and barely animated. It was obvious they were being restrained by something powerful.

Reivn saw them and turned. "How long can you hold them?"

The strain was already showing on the Epochian's face, as tiny beads of blood ran down his forehead. "Not long!" he groaned.

"Stay with me and give me every second you can!" Reivn shouted. Then he sent a telepathy to the members of Djordji's team who were still alive. *Hold fast! We're coming!* Letting loose a barrage of lightning that was almost blinding in its intensity, he yelled to the rest of his team. "Follow me!"

His assault gave the warriors behind him an open channel to fill, and they pressed forward, cutting down the daemons that barred their path. The Mithranians paired off with their Thylacinian counterparts, so that as one was engaging the other was dispatching. The Dracanas followed suit. The Sargonians followed, focused on wielding their wraiths to aid their forward progress. It was efficient and produced deadly results. The wedge they were cutting through the lesser beasts widened with every stroke of their blades.

The other teams followed his example, utilizing the strengths of each tribe's birthrights and compensating for their weaknesses. Their teams began to fight with renewed zeal, cutting through the monsters with ferocity until finally, they reached Reivn's side and joined forces.

Reivn nodded to Lucian and Leshye, and then turned and yelled, "Mithranians, Thylacinians... to the front, Sargonians, Epochians... to the sides! Dracanas, Mastrics, to the rear and cover our advance! Form a dual-lined triangle and shield wall! Push forward to Djordji's team! Move!"

Lucian's team moved into place beside Leshye's, and Marcus quickly joined them with what was left of his. The group spread out to an almost perfect triangle, bringing up their shields and weapons to defend from all angles as they began their advance.

Reivn kept the Epochian who was holding the daemon warriors at bay in the center to protect him. Worried they would not get across the field before the daemon warriors broke free, he stayed close to the front and fought alongside his men to help them move faster.

The Epochian's eyes were weeping blood as he strained to hold them back and was clearly in pain, but he refused to yield, recognizing that the survival of their entire group now depended on him. However, the strain proved to be too great, and he lost consciousness and collapsed.

The second the daemon warriors were free, they turned their magic on him, obliterating his body from the inside out.

"NO!" Reivn shouted, horrified by the man's fate, the deep-seated guilt he felt at having led him to his death ripping though him.

There was no time for regret as the daemon warriors descended on them, unleashing hellfire and pure dark energy.

Two of the Mastrics at the back of the group immediately raised kinetic shields to protect those who were left, while the rest launched lightning and pure holy light at the five monsters whose total attention was now on them.

Reivn could see the bedraggled remains of Djordji's team struggling to hold their ground just a few yards away. All around them were the shredded bodies of their comrades and the daemons they had managed to kill, and they were using these as a wall to put between them and their attackers, who now outnumbered them.

Disgusted that so many had been sacrificed in a mere test for command skills by the Ancients, who sat watching as though this were a spectator sport, Reivn spun around with sudden deliberation. "Lucian, Leshye, lead them the rest of the way and get to Djordji's men! I will cover you!"

Lucian nodded and signaled Leshye. Then he took the lead and tightened their ranks, while Reivn moved to the back of the group and summoned the Spirals, tapping into the magic Mastric had filled him with earlier that night.

However, Leshye hesitated, looking over her shoulder at Reivn. *He's willing to die out there rather than lose anyone else... I cannot let him stand alone.* Her decision made, she turned abruptly and left the line, pushing her way through those around her to get to Reivn's side.

"What are you doing?" Reivn asked her, caught off-guard by her sudden appearance at his side.

She smiled and pushed her hat back a little as she braced herself for the coming fight. "What I was trained to do!"

There was no more time for conversation. The daemon warriors descended on them with a vengeance, their shrieks of fury filling the night sky. Their sights were set on Reivn because he had denied them their prey.

Reivn drove his right heel into the ground behind him and dove as deep into the Spirals as he dared, and when they were almost on top of him, he unleashed a powerful blast of pure light, infused with the power of Heaven's grace... the one gift he had inherited at birth, and the one gift that could turn the tide in this fight.

It hit two of the flying beasts head on, blowing through their wings so hot it melted them. They plummeted to the ground, unable to stay aloft.

Leshye did not hesitate. She dove forward and turned into a whirling dervish of moving blades, cutting into them with a speed that even among the first generation was a rarity. She was blindingly fast and hit with deadly accuracy.

Behind them, Lucian, Marcus and the rest of the group had reached Djordji's men. Now they were working together to kill the daemons that remained on the ground.

Then the remaining daemon warriors swooped down for another round.

Leshye saw them just in time and dropped to the ground, rolling out of their grasp.

Worried she was too close to them, Reivn leaped forward, grabbing her by her arms and dragging her to safety. Then he shielded her while she got to her feet. The seconds that followed went by in a blur as he was snatched into the air by two of the three remaining beasts. Shouts went up, there was a sudden powerful blast of energy, and then he was falling. He slammed into the hard ground head-first and knew nothing more.

# THE BLOODLINE

## Chapter Eleven
## Debt Honored

"Reivn..."

Reivn's ears were ringing and all he could feel was pain. His eyes did not want to open, and the warmth that ran down the side of his face felt sticky and wet.

"Reivn. Wake up. You are needed here." Leshye dabbed at the blood on his brow. "I think he's coming around, " she said, looking up at Lucian.

Lucian nodded and glanced at his companions in relief.

Annie, Darius, Lazar and Alderion had all come down from the pavilion in the minutes that followed Reivn's fall and were standing around him worriedly.

"What..." Reivn muttered, opening his eyes and trying to focus. "What happened?"

Chuckling in relief, Lucian knelt beside him. "You saved Leshye's life and almost bit it yourself. I've never seen anything like that. You shielded her with your own body. I suppose Mastric didn't like the daemons going after you because he ended the fight the moment you were snatched up. You both would have died had he not destroyed them."

Leshye glared at him. "Shut up, Lucian. I could have handled it! I did not need his help!" she snapped.

"Yes, we all saw how well you were handled," Annie snickered. "That I should be that lucky. Relax. You had two daemon warriors on you. None of us could have taken them on alone like you tried to. Reivn saved your life. There's no shame in that."

Lucian growled and lowered his voice. "The only shame is that we had to fight in the first place."

Loudly clearing his throat to cover what Lucian was saying, Darius placed his hand on Lucian's shoulder, reminding him they were not alone. "Perhaps it is best you leave that thought for another time," he quietly suggested.

Reivn could feel the damage in his body and knew he was seriously injured. "I could not let another of you die." He struggled to sit up.

Lucian held him down. "You need a Cleric's attention, brother. Rest easy."

Reivn pushed his arm away. "I will see a Cleric once we are done here. There are unsettled matters at hand and a decision still needs to be made." He forced himself to sit up, fighting off the dizziness and accompanying nauseousness that followed the waves of pain flooding his senses. "We must select a Commander-in-Chief among ourselves or they will be the death of us all," he added, stifling a groan.

Darius stood silent for a second before nodding his head as he thought of a solution. "I believe we have already selected someone." He glanced at his fellow Warlords and raised an eyebrow, a question in his eyes. Then he dropped to his left knee in front of Reivn, crossing his right fist across his chest in a show of respect.

One by one the other Warlords joined him, honoring Reivn as their new leader.

From the pavilion above, a shout rang out. "You would select the man whose brother killed Arian?" Mithras was enraged they dared to pay Reivn homage as they were. Then his eyes beheld Leshye, and he sobered.

Sharrukin did not miss his expression. "Your daughter would have been slaughtered had Reivn not intervened, risking his own life to do so. If this is the measure of the man they have chosen, they have made a wise choice indeed."

From beneath his hood, Mastric's unseen smile was cold and calculating. He was pleased with his son. "He will make an excellent leader. That was quite a show. Had he not led them as he did, more of your children would have died."

Galatia glared at him. "Had you not summoned something as foul as those Daemon warriors, none of our children would have died... only the warriors you gave them to use. Djordji's blood is on your hands!"

Tired of the bickering and recognizing that regardless of his tribe, Reivn had been the best leader on the field, Victus raised a hand to his forehead in exasperation. "Enough! All of you! The Warlords all support him, and he did in fact win the challenge! It is decided!" Then he turned to Silvanus, who sat silently brooding in his seat. "I am sorry about your son, Silvanus. His was another tragic loss. His skills will be missed on the battlefield."

Silvanus held up his hand reluctantly. "I was the fool who put him on the field to fight. His death is my fault. I was not prepared to trust Reivn after Valfort's repeat offenses, and I was wrong. We should not have judged him because of his brother's deeds. Djordji paid for the rash decision we all made. I will be a few nights trying to decide who among my children must replace him as Warlord for the Dracanas. Has anyone summoned the Clerics to see to the injuries of the survivors?"

"I did," Armenia admitted in irritation. "Marcus has already stated his desire to follow Reivn after his actions tonight. So, we concede on the choice of leadership."

Sharrukin got up. "Well, I for one, am going down there to speak to that young man. Lazar thinks highly of him after his performance tonight, as do I. I want to know more about him."

"Annie has work to do, and I am not inclined to speak with him in his present state. I will meet him again when he next comes to court." Galatia glanced at Victus as she got up. "I am retiring for the night. Annie knows her way home, and I am bored with this bickering, so I bid you all a good night." Without waiting for a response, she vanished, teleporting to the lower levels of the fortress and her own chambers.

From his spot on the cold stone floor, Thylacinos snickered and stretched. "She does hate to lose." Then he yawned and scratched his head, growling in frustration. He had wanted Reivn to fail, but even he had to admit the Mastric Warlord had exceeded his expectations. "The whelp does seem to lead well," he said grudgingly. "...and he did watch out for my children instead of making them cannon fodder. So perhaps he is the right choice."

The crowd was already dispersing, and Victus watched them in silence until Mithras got his attention.

"I am going to take my leave as well. Leshye will no doubt remain with her fellow Warlords until Reivn is on his feet again, but I do not need to coddle her. She is quite adept at defending herself." Mithras stared at her for a minute before getting up to leave. *The decision was made, Leshye,* he telepathied. *Reivn will take Arian's place. Come home when you are ready. You did well tonight.*

Leshye briefly looked up at the pavilion and her father. Then she turned back to helping Reivn in silence.

Sharrukin approached the Warlords respectfully, his wise eyes noting the hope in theirs. Then he looked down at the man who had given it to them. "You are quite a remarkable young man, Reivn," he observed, his weathered features creasing into a smile. "I have not heard much of you, but I look forward to following your career in the future. Our people need a strong leader, and we lost that when Arian died. You have shown you have that ability in what you accomplished tonight. You did well."

Gazing up at the Ancient in surprise, Reivn frowned. "I assumed the Council would be displeased when I broke the rules of engagement for the challenge. You are not angry?"

"On the contrary, young man. I am pleased more of you did not die. I believed this challenge to have been quite unnecessary, which is why Lazar did not participate. We do not need to grab for power. It has a way of finding true leaders on its own." He smiled and bowed again before walking away, leaving Reivn to stare after him in confusion.

Lucian gazed down at their new Commander-in-Chief. He had never met Reivn before tonight but had heard of his skill in battle. He realized now that the rumors were understated. The man lying on the ground in front of him was not only skilled, but a seasoned and formidable warrior. Yet he had shown them all mercy, and offered aid when none was expected, risking his own status by defying the rules of the test. *He is nothing like his father. Is it possible he truly is the best choice for us? Perhaps we can finally begin to minimize our losses under his command.* He watched as the Cleric worked on him, his mind full of questions. *I hope you are the man we believe you to be, Reivn*, he telepathied.

"Lucian," Reivn replied, looking up at him. "I do not know what kind of mettle is in me, but I swear to you. As long as I lead, I will never abandon any of you. The trust you have placed in me will be met with honor and the respect you all deserve."

Recognizing the worth of such a promise, Lucian knelt again and clasped Reivn's hand in a firm grip. "It is a pleasure to meet you, brother." Darius tapped his shoulder, interrupting him, and he glanced up in time to see Thylacinos loping toward him. He quickly got to his feet, worried his father would be angry with him.

"I see you accepted the Mastric," Thylacinos rumbled as he drew near. "I suppose it is just as well. It has been decided up there. Reivn is the new Commander-in-Chief. We shall see if he can continue what he began here tonight." He gazed down at the Mastric Warlord for a minute as though he would say more, and then snorted and walked away. "I am for the hunt!"

Visibly relaxing, Lucian smiled at Reivn before turning to follow his father.

The Cleric finished with Reivn, and Darius offered him a hand up. "Welcome to the team, Reivn," he stated with a smile.

The other Warlords crowded around him, congratulating him one at a time and offering what advice they could.

Reivn glanced up at the pavilion as he listened and caught Mastric's gaze. He quickly looked away again, knowing his father was pleased. The discomfort he felt under such scrutiny made the hairs on his neck stand up. He tried to shake it off, but then the Warlords fell silent and he turned to see Mastric gliding toward them. "Father..." he bowed respectfully.

Mastric waved the other Warlords away. "Come, Reivn. We have other matters to discuss that will not wait."

Darius immediately nodded to Leshye, Marcus and the others, and they walked away, leaving Reivn and Mastric alone. None of them wanted to anger the Ancient.

Waiting until they were out of earshot, Mastric chuckled and gripped Reivn's shoulder. "Well done, my boy. Well done. You exceeded my expectations tonight. Even Valfort could not have done so well."

"I did not do it for you, father," Reivn said stiffly, not caring if his words brought repercussions. "I was not going to stand by and watch any more of them get cut down like that... not when I knew how to save them."

Mastric's eyes narrowed. "Stupid child! This test was not about saving anyone! It was about how well you could lead, and you proved you could outthink them all under the stress of combat!"

Reivn turned to meet his father's gaze. "That tends to happen when you spend centuries struggling to survive on one battlefield after another. But tell me, my lord... did you intentionally summon those daemon warriors that killed Djordji tonight?"

"I think you already know the answer to that. He should have been more careful." Mastric eyed his son in silence for a minute. "Your new rank puts you in a position where I can no longer send you on personal missions. However, remember this... I have your son, and his survival depends on your continued cooperation. Step wrong and he dies. He will do my personal missions from now on, but he will be on a far shorter leash than you ever were, and his life will be in your hands."

Bowing low, Reivn realized that even in his present position, Mastric wanted to make him a puppet. He closed his eyes, dreading future nights and what this meant for his growing family. "I will be as I always have... loyal and obedient to the Alliance."

Mastric eyed him carefully, sensing his growing resentment. "You are very important to me, Reivn... you and your sons. We have a significant future ahead of us, and much we need to accomplish. But I can only protect you as long as you follow my lead. I should warn you, should you think about stepping out of line, as Valfort has done, I cannot guarantee Lunitar would not gain the knowledge his village was a mere sacrifice for the real goal of securing him. Are you certain he will forgive you for that, concerning who you killed in the process?"

Reivn looked up and stared at him in shock. "You told me that attack was necessary because the Principatus used the town as a base! You said we needed to find him to prevent him from being a part of it! I was following your orders!"

"Ah yes... my orders. I told you to raid the village. I said nothing about killing all those in it, did I?" Mastric grinned, knowing he had Reivn cornered.

Shaking his head, Reivn gazed at his hands, remembering the blood on them that night. "You said to be sure there were no witnesses."

Mastric laughed then. "Yes... make sure there were no witnesses, not to leave no witnesses. You could have just moved through the darkness and captured him. You chose instead to destroy the village."

"Only because it was what your orders implied! Why did you not clarify? You could have stopped me!" Reivn grew angry, his resentment at how he had been manipulated growing stronger with every word. "Did you intend for me to kill Lunitar as well?"

Mastric grabbed Reivn's hand and held it up, pointing out the ring on his finger... the crest of the Draegon family for centuries. "You wanted your name restored amongst the nobles of your people. I gave you that and more. You brought Lunitar back and begged me to spare him, remember? Whether or not I intended you to do so is irrelevant. He is here and you have turned him. That is what he knows. As long as you remain loyal, it is all he will ever know. Any sanctity your family has remains intact as long as you continue as you have tonight. Remember your duties, Warlord..." His voice faded as he disappeared into the black mist, leaving Reivn standing on the field alone to stare at the carnage around him.

Reivn could not bring himself to return home right away, so he took the room reserved for the Mastric's Warlord in Polusporta, shutting himself away for several nights, horrified at what he had learned. He thought of the trust he had been given by Lunitar and Seth both, and how miserably he had failed them, and he hated himself for it. Remaining in his room, he paced the floor night after night, trying to find a way out of the trap Mastric had set for him and berating himself for being such a fool.

Then one night, Sharrukin knocked on his door.

Reivn threw it open, not sure who to expect. He drew a quick intake of breath when he recognized the Ancient. "My apologies, my lord. I did not know it was you. Please... come in."

Sharrukin bowed and entered. Then he turned and faced the young Warlord. "I will get right to the point of my visit. I know not why you have chosen to hide here instead of returning home, but I can tell you that whatever the problem you face, it will not disappear because you stay here. Sooner or later, you must return to your family and face them. You will know what to say and when to say it. Trust your instincts. I believe they will guide you well."

Reivn dropped his gaze. "I did not think to be that obvious, my lord. You shame me. I am... struggling with my new position and how this will change everything for them."

"We both know that is only half of it," Sharrukin observed shrewdly. "I know your father's penchant for cruelty. I saw the two of you on the field that night. I do not know what passed between you, but I know my brother well enough to understand your fear. Go home, Reivn. Lead our armies to many victories and build a name for yourself. This alone will give you the power to fight back. Now, I take my leave. Farewell for now, Dragon lord."

Reivn stared at the door long after Sharrukin was gone, thinking over what he had said, and recognizing the truth in his words. *Dragon lord?* He was confused over that one. Then he thought, *Build my reputation and name... such a daunting task.* He realized what it meant for all of them. Then he thought about what Mastric had revealed about Lunitar, and a familiar knot formed in his stomach. He valued the relationship he had built with the man he now called his son. Mastric's revelation threatened all of it... everything he cherished. Then he realized what Sharrukin had said was true. Sooner or later, he would have to return to Draegonstorm and face his sons. He was only delaying the inevitable. "Build my name..." he whispered to the empty room. His jaw clenched with determination, he opened the door and headed to the portal chamber.

# THE BLOODLINE

## Chapter Twelve
## Warlord's Rise

Reivn was far longer returning home than planned, and Lunitar was worried. He said nothing to Gideon about his concerns, knowing it would only serve to upset him, but as the nights passed, he would often stop by the portal room, only to be told it had remained silent. *I knew this was going to be a long process, but I didn't think it would be this long. There's far more going on here than the selection of a Commander-in-Chief. Who am I kidding? This is a decision that could greatly impact the Alliance for the next millennium or longer. It will impact our family as well, in more ways than one, no matter the outcome.* He headed to the library again, as he had every night since his father's departure, his thoughts very dark. However, when he sat down to read, he was too distracted and stared at the pages without really seeing them.

Gideon found him there a couple of hours later and dropped into a chair beside him. "Didn't you hear me?" he asked, sounding concerned. "I have been talking to you for the last ten minutes. I was looking all over for you, though I should have known you would be here!"

"I am sorry, brother. Father's continued absence has frankly got me worried. It's been far longer than I imagined it would be." Lunitar pushed the book away and leaned back in his chair in frustration.

Gideon sat silent for a moment, thinking about their predicament. "What if he doesn't return?" he finally asked, doubt filling his voice.

Lunitar stared at him. He had not even thought of that. Then he shoved the idea aside and shook his head. "If he does not return, you and I will have a lot of work to do, but I am sure he will. It's just a matter of when. A Warlord's replacement is known to take some time. I imagine the selection of the Commander-in-Chief must be far more difficult."

"It was indeed difficult," Reivn said from the door as he walked in. "...but not for the reasons you think. I thought I might find you both here. Come. We have much to discuss tonight."

At the sight of him, Lunitar jumped up, knocking over his chair. "You have returned! Thank God!" he exclaimed, breathing a sigh of relief.

Gideon quickly got up, grinning ear to ear. "I knew you were too tough to be taken down! Welcome home, father!"

Reivn walked over to join them and stopped at Gideon's side. "You have been on my mind much of late," he replied and hugged his son. "We have matters to settle between us. However, you must both know what has occurred first. Come."

Lunitar and Gideon quickly joined him, and they headed for the Commonroom.

On the way, Reivn listened as Lunitar gave his full report on the activities at the Keep.

Gideon walked beside them in silence, lost in his own thoughts. His father's greeting had been very unexpected, but it had been most welcome, and his hopes had risen that maybe they were finally healing old wounds.

Reivn noted his silence and briefly rested his hand on his son's shoulder, giving it a reassuring squeeze before letting go.

Seeing this, Lunitar smiled to himself. There was definitely change in the air. Then his thoughts turned to what Reivn wanted to discuss, and he grew worried. He knew Mastric's penchant for cruelty and wondered if something had happened.

When they entered the Commonroom, Reivn closed the door and locked it behind them. Then he motioned for them both to sit down while he walked over to the bar. Pulling out three glasses, he filled them with rum, and then quickly dropped a few drops of his own blood in each before turning and carrying them to where his sons waited for him.

Gideon took his glass without a word.

However, Lunitar glanced first at the door, then at his glass, and raised an eyebrow as he turned to stare at Reivn. "Father?" His voice filled with questions he could not ask.

Reivn sat down across from them. "This was not a trip I ever expected to make, and it has changed everything... our roles in society, our responsibilities... our very lives." He downed his drink and slammed his glass down on the table. "It would seem Mastric has far bigger plans than I realized, but I do not yet know what those plans are or how they involve us. Make no mistake, however. They do involve us... considerably."

Gideon frowned, Reivn's words weighing heavy on him. "What has happened, father? Have you been appointed Commander-in-Chief?"

Sitting forward, Lunitar almost held his breath as he waited for Reivn's response.

Reivn nodded and got up. Walking back to the bar, he poured himself another drink and laced it in record time. Then he turned around. "When I first arrived at the Guild, Mastric demanded my presence to reveal his plans before we headed to Polusporta for the meeting with the Council. It would seem Valfort made one too many mistakes. Mastric informed me that Arian's death was his fault, because he ignored Arian's pleas for help. And this time, the Council would not allow him to remain the Mastric's Warlord. So, I am not just the Commander-in-Chief of the Alliance armies. I am now also the Mastric's Warlord. Valfort was demoted and severely punished for his disobedience." He drained his glass again and put it down. "This family has just been thrust to the very forefront of this war."

"On both fronts it would seem..." Lunitar added uncomfortably, emptying his own glass before walking over to set it beside his father's. "So not only are we now at the forefront of the war with the Principatus, we have been thrust to the front of the political battlefield as well... and either one could just as easily destroy us."

Reivn growled in frustration. "Destroy us... no... he will not allow that. He has plans for us." He walked over and dropped into a chair opposite the hearth and stared at the fire in silence.

Lunitar exchanged glances with Gideon, wondering what he was not telling them.

"Father," Gideon spoke quietly, as though afraid he would incur Reivn's wrath. "If Mastric has designs on you or this family, then perhaps it is well that you do indeed rise in power. As Prince of this territory, your authority has always been limited to this location, but as a Warlord, that restriction has been lifted. Mayhap this is to your advantage?"

Only listening with half an ear, Reivn almost did not hear him, his own thoughts distracting him as he mulled over all Mastric had said. He sat in silence, staring at the fire, seeing a village in flames and hearing the screams of the dying. In his heart, he knew he could not tell Lunitar the truth... not now.

"I agree with Gideon, Father," Lunitar added. "You and I have spoken at length many times about what we wanted to accomplish, but we always lacked two very important things... opportunity and authority. Now one of those obstacles has been removed."

Reivn looked up then, realizing he was right. "I have been so distracted since my appointment that I honestly had not thought of that. You know me, Lunitar. I have always believed the higher the rank, the greater the power. The greater the power, the more it corrupts you. I would rather serve a Commander than be one."

Understanding his fear, Lunitar nodded. "If any man can survive the corruption of advancement in our society, father, it is you. And since we're being honest, I will do everything in my power to prevent you from being anything other than yourself."

"As will I," Gideon got up to stand beside his brother.

Lunitar smiled at him and continued. "As it appears I speak for both of us... then know this father. Not only am I your son, I am also your friend. I will have your back as long as I draw breath."

Determination filling his face, Gideon agreed. "And as long as I draw breath, you will never stand alone."

Reivn got up slowly, his expression grim, and his eyes took on a darker hue as they filled with new purpose. "Then let us form a pact. The oath I hold to... let it become your own. Let us stand together as father and sons, and brothers in arms from this day forward. Swear your oath to our banners and hold to our creed... Fealty, wisdom, and above all... honor.

Lunitar knelt on his left knee and placed his right fist over his chest. "Honor... fealty... wisdom... I, Lunitar Draegon, do so swear to uphold this code and our family name until my final breath."

Quickly joining him, Gideon bowed his head as he knelt. "Honor, fealty, and wisdom. I, Gideon Draegon swear to serve you father, and this family until I draw my last breath."

Walking over to place his hands on their shoulders, Reivn whispered, "So be it. Rise, my sons. From this day forth, you bear the crest of our noble house and fight at my side to defend humanity and the Alliance against our enemies. The world shall know the Draegon name. Allies shall honor it and enemies shall quake in fear at our passing. Our banners shall fly above the battlefield and lead our armies to victory. The dawn of the Dragon has come."

From out in the hall, Alora pulled away from the door as silently as she had rested against it. Then she straightened up with a smile and her dark eyes flashed dangerously. *So... it turns out that indulging him in his desire for me has paid off. The dawn of the dragon indeed. Your fire will burn every tribe to ashes before I am through with you. Finally... the tool to rid me of those cumbersome Ancients guarding humanity is mine... delivered in the cloak of a Warlord with the power of a Commander-in-Chief. He's as good as wrapped in chains and delivered to my feet.*

She slipped silently down the hall, delighted at the news, immediately beginning to plan how she would tighten her grip on him. *I must make sure no one can come between us and the only way to do that is to marry the fool. Fortunately for me, he's at least handsome and more than a little appealing. I can amuse myself with him for as long as it takes to achieve the destruction of the Alliance.* Laughing at how fortune had favored her, she slipped into her room unnoticed and closed the door.

Unaware they had been eavesdropped on, Reivn continued talking with his sons, his concern with the future weighing heavily on his mind. He voiced several worries about their new roles, wanting them to know exactly what they were up against. However, he kept Mastric's true involvement to himself. As they spoke, he stared at Lunitar, stunned at his own part in the deception.

Lunitar was focused on what his duties would be and completely missed just how distraught Reivn actually was over his trip with Mastric. He sat deep in thought, staring at the fire as he mulled over their future until finally, he looked up. "So, if I understand this right, with you assuming the roles of the Mastric's Warlord and the Commander-in-Chief, Gideon's and my martial responsibilities will increase. So, how do you wish us to proceed here, father?"

Reivn was silent for a moment. Then he said, "First off, that letter you bear, Lunitar... open it and send it to the Council so it is registered. I need officers I can trust, and as of yet, I do not know how many if any will be that loyal. I will provide a similar letter for Gideon, though to a lesser rank." Then he glanced at Gideon. "This is not a slight to you. Because I have not yet released you, placing you too high could cause a problem with the Council. I also do not know what I will face from our soldiers yet or what kind of loyalty they will have."

"Are you honestly so concerned they may not accept you?" Gideon stared at his father in surprise. "Somehow, I cannot imagine they could or would do anything else. There is a good chance the Council would flay the hides from anyone who dared dispute their decision."

"If there is even a question that some would not accept or follow him, then I know my first order of business," Lunitar interjected. "...and that will be determining who is loyal to you, and who is not. I can segregate them by creating the Warlord's personal guard. Then over time, I will be able to remove those who are not and replace them with new recruits."

Reivn shook his head. "I think it would be wiser to form my personal guard from those here at Draegonstorm. They have already proven their loyalty a thousand times over. I can have you oversee the appropriate promotions for that purpose." Then he paused. "However, if we are forming a personal guard for me, we would have to change their title. The Honor Guard has been a time honored tradition here at Draegonstorm, and something many warriors have vied with each other to join. I do not wish to strip them of that honor."

Lunitar stared at the fire as he thought about it. Finally, he said, "We could just change it slightly, making the title for the main battalion more geared toward your crest and the Keep. We could call the fortress Guard the Dragon Guard and name each division within it to identify those of higher rank from lower.

"I like the idea of calling them the Dragon Guard," Gideon added eagerly. "The family crest is, after all, twin combatant Dragons. So it makes sense."

Reivn looked from one to the other and slowly nodded, liking the idea. "It would give them the sense of change they will need now that I have risen so much in rank, while preserving the original Guard itself. The highest ranked division would be the Elite Guard, as they would serve as the family's personal Guard. The others will be the Crimson, Black, and Standard Guards, after our crest colors. Those who have been here serving loyally long term could be broken down into officers, non-coms and enlisted and assigned in each of the other divisions to spread them equally across the ranks. This way each position is part of an honored division and has loyal soldiers among their numbers. Over time, they will develop their own traditions through friendly competitions."

Lunitar listened intently, making mental notes on where he wanted to start organizing them. "I think the Standard Guard should be used for the incoming soldiers as a means of identifying the new from those who have been here for a long time." Wondering where he fit into this, he pulled out Reivn's letter, broke the seal, and quickly read its contents. Then he looked up in concern. "You were serious about making me a Commander? Will the Council agree to such a high rank when I am so newly released?"

With a chuckle, Reivn got up and walked over to stoke the fire. "Yes. They are leaving all those decisions to me. Apparently, they have no interest in how I run the armies, as long as I get the results they want. However, if I should fail, I will suffer for it."

Gideon shifted nervously. "Where would you want me, father? I know you do not think I am Commander material yet."

Lunitar glanced at him. "Maybe not, but you would be a good captain under me," he said with a smile.

"Agreed," Reivn stated. "You would actually make a very good captain, and in time a good Commander. You have the fortitude and tenacity, just not the experience. That is the only thing holding you back right now. Your Roman father did you no favors by keeping you at home."

"Well then it's settled. He'll be my captain. It will be my duty to train him up as my replacement," Lunitar grinned. "So young captain, you had best keep your eyes and ears open, and your mouth shut except to ask pertinent questions. We might make a Commander out of you yet."

Gideon frowned. "Is that all the time or just on the field? I don't fancy being subordinate to you here at home. That seems a bit awkward." He gazed at Reivn as he spoke, his eyes asking more than he was saying.

Reivn realized Gideon was worried about not being accepted and patted his shoulder in reassurance. "Here at home, you are both my sons and rank matters not unless I say it does. If we cannot have this refuge from our duties than where?"

Gideon looked visibly relieved. "Thank you, father. I will do my best to serve as a good captain and make you both proud."

## Chapter Thirteen
## Second Son

The next two weeks were spent restructuring the ranks already stationed at Draegonstorm. Reivn had assigned the interviews and placement of personnel to Lunitar, while Gideon worked with the Quartermaster to commission new supplies to meet the needs of incoming soldiers when they arrived and issuing new uniforms to their current troops.

Reivn was handling the search for new recruits and sending the necessary letters to transfer or recruit new soldiers. His goal was to have a complete battalion before the month's end. He knew that before long, he would have to formally address all the Alliance officers to officially make himself known. So while he worked on the recruitment list, he also began plans for the assembly of all Alliance officers to take place at Draegonstorm. When he could no longer delay setting a date, he summoned Lunitar to his office to make the necessary arrangements.

Lunitar knocked and poked his head in. "You sent for me, father?"

Looking up, Reivn nodded. "Yes. We need to discuss the formal introduction to my officers. I am planning to hold it here at the Keep and must set a date. So we need to discuss security."

"Very well, father. However, I need writing utensils, so I will return shortly." Lunitar turned to leave.

Reivn stopped him and handed him a bundle. "Here. I knew you would need them, so I took the liberty of sending for them prior to summoning you."

Lunitar chuckled and sat down. "So, will I be arranging for a formal ball as well? How big of an event will this be?"

"It is not going to be anything other than the necessary meeting in the throne room. However, we still do not know which way any of these officers intends to lean. So I do not think it wise to take any chances. We are nearing completion of the Dragon Guard. So they need to be ready for that night." Reivn handed him several lists. "Here are the final names of those I secured for duty here. They will all be here by the week's end. Can you have them settled before the end of the month."

Lunitar began looking over the lists. "I can have them either settled and trained or gotten rid of by the end of the month. I will get these lists to the Quartermaster and ensure they have the appropriate equipment and uniforms issued upon their arrival."

Reivn nodded in satisfaction. "Good. Now, we will need Guards posted at every strategic location within the Keep, and we will need a healthy contingent in the throne room as well. I am just trying to decide how many I want in there, so as not to insult my officers, while maintaining a strong presence." He looked uncomfortable for a moment. "I am not used to having to put on a show this way."

"It is always easier to enter as a Lion and relax your restrictions than to enter as a lamb and try to increase your hold on them later." Lunitar reminded him. "I believe two full platoons would be appropriate, with the remainder of the company on duty throughout the Keep. And frankly, if there is going to be an attempt on your life, they may see this meeting as the perfect time to do so. Most don't know you yet, and they do not know what you are capable of. That ignorance might lead some to believe they can take full advantage of being in such a close proximity to you. With that in mind, would it not be wise to have the other Warlords in attendance as well?"

Reivn looked as though he had been struck. "I had not even thought of them. The Warlords should of course be here. This is, after all, basically a change of command, albeit a forced one due to Arian's demise. Having them here could encourage a smoother transition to my command and perhaps discourage those who have little faith in my abilities to lead them." He paused before continuing, a troubled look on his face. "I never imagined I would ever be thrust into this high of a position. I do not want it, yet here I am, and I absolutely cannot fail. The price for that failure would be too high."

Lunitar stared at him, noting his discomfort. "I know there is a lot at stake here, father... I'm willing to bet far more than you're willing to tell me. However, if I am going to be your second, and effectively execute that role, I need to know what to expect. And you have hand-picked everyone in the Dragon Guard without exception because you trust them, but you cannot trust their Commander with the entire truth? That does not bode well for a good start."

"I do trust you, Lunitar," Reivn began, searching for the right words to comfort his son. "...with the full measure of all I am. Mastric demands absolute obedience. You know this. He told me that night I would be the new Commander-in-Chief before we ever set foot in the Council's halls. This means he planned to have me take this position regardless of the consequences. He only does this when he has plans that involve us directly. I cannot say what those plans are, but I do know his wrath, as do you. You know if I fail him, none will be spared."

"That is true," Lunitar agreed. "So do as you always do, and you will not fail him. And I will do as I have always done... ensuring that you are successful."

Reivn gazed at Lunitar fondly, relieved he had accepted that as the only reason for his discomfort. He was not prepared to explain anything else yet. "I do not regret making you my son. It was the best gift I could ever have been given. Now, let us get to work on the details..."

The night of the formal Change of Command arrived and the halls of Draegonstorm were bustling with activity. Every strategic location in the fortress was manned by Guards and the Keep was heavily reinforced. The patrols had been doubled, and in the throne room, Guards had been stationed not only around the perimeter, but also in a formation of two columns leading up to the throne itself. New livery and uniforms had been turned out for every Guard member and servant, and there had been nights of cleaning in preparation for the event.

Reivn stood in his chambers being assisted by servants with his armor and formal tunic. As they dressed him, he stared at the wall, deep in thought. Then a knock at the door shook him back to the present. He glanced over his shoulder. "Come!"

The door opened and Lunitar walked in. "My lord, all preparations are complete, and the guests are arriving. I am here with your personal contingent to escort you to the throne room."

Reivn nodded and turned. "This is it then. Tonight, we change history. I am now committed to this and must not fail." His expression was not nearly as confident as he sounded. The worry in his eyes betrayed him.

"If I may be so bold, my lord... do you need more time to prepare?" Lunitar knew he was uncertain and was concerned it would be obvious to those awaiting his arrival in the throne room. "I hear your conviction, but it's reflection is distorted in your expression."

Reivn shook his head. "No. More time will not alleviate the pressure Mastric has placed on my shoulders. Whether now or later, it will still be there. I must simply use the discipline Mastric taught us and bury any emotions. I am ready."

Lunitar looked him over with a critical eye, tugging on his armor to ensure it was properly secured. Then nodding in satisfaction, he said, "Well then... in review, we will proceed with the change of command, and then the banquet to follow. As we previously discussed, all guests who wish to retain their weapons will be allowed to do so."

"The Warlords will ensure their own people assist with keeping the guests in line," Reivn reminded him. "And should anyone try to cause trouble, armed or no, I am quite able to deal with them myself." He sighed and shook his head. "God, I sound like my father. And yet, I know it is necessary. They must fear me to a certain extent in order to respect me. If they think I am not strong enough to lead them, they will never accept me, much less follow me into battle." He clenched his jaw, and his eyes filled with determination.

There was another knock at the door.

"Come!" Reivn commanded.

Gideon poked his head in. "Father? The guests are all accounted for. Are you ready?" Then he saw his brother. " Ah, good evening Lunitar. I saw the escort in the hall. They look good." He grinned and strode in. "I know I'm supposed to walk down there with you, but are you sure you don't want me to go on ahead just to be sure all is well?"

"No, Gideon," Reivn said, correcting him. "You will walk in with me and your brother. This event is being held in our home, and you are a Lord of Draegonstorm. As such, it falls under the same rules as royalty. You are the son of the ruler here, so you will walk as such. The other officers will handle everything else." Then he glanced at Lunitar. "Shall we?"

In response, Lunitar walked over and opened the door for him. "After you, my lord." He smiled at Gideon as Reivn walked by and then together, they stepped out after him.

They arrived at the throne room to a bustling of activity. The Guards outside the entrance quickly crossed their right fists over their chests before opening the massive oak double doors. Guests were standing around talking quietly, but the chatter ceased the moment they opened.

Lunitar entered first, followed by Gideon. They took three measured strides before quickly side-stepping, one to the right and the other left. Then in unison, they turned and faced each other. "Dragons to!" Lunitar commanded. He had augmented his voice with the Spirals, so it would echo throughout the room and the rest of the fortress.

Immediately, Lunitar, Gideon and every other soldier in the Keep lifted their right arms as one and crossed them over their chest in salute.

Then Lunitar announced, "My lords, ladies, and assembled guests... I present to you the lord of Draegonstorm, progenitor of the Draegon line, Prince of the Australian territories, Warlord of the Mastric tribe, and Commander-in-Chief of the Alliance forces, Lord Reivn Christoff Demitri Draegon."

Reivn stepped forward and entered the room, his face expressionless. Nodding slightly to his sons, he walked through the center column of his guards, his eyes on the throne ahead. He knew if he acknowledged anyone at this crucial moment, it would be seen as favoritism, so he made a point of keeping his eyes forward. He slowly climbed the steps and then turned.

Lunitar and Gideon had followed him, keeping exactly two measured steps behind him at all times until he sat down. Then Lunitar moved to stand at his right, while Gideon stood at his left.

Reivn looked around at the assembled officers and guests. "Welcome to Draegonstorm. Let me start by thanking you all for coming. I know many of you were busy with other duties and had to make arrangements in order to attend. So, I will keep this short for all our sakes. You all know I have been appointed as your new Commander-in-Chief. I will not waste time by telling you of the challenge the Warlords underwent for this position. It is enough they have endorsed my appointment. Many of you no doubt question whether or not I am able to fulfill the duties of this position. Rest assured, I am not only capable, I have already begun to implement strategic changes to our military structure. Some of you may have noticed a sudden shift in ranks among your numbers. This is because I have been evaluating all of you as officers, and those directly beneath you to ensure each of you are where you can perform at your best." He paused to let that sink in. Then he continued. "I have noticed the practice of keeping some tribes in lower ranks only, while promoting others who are not capable of handling the positions they are given. This must change. I know it may not necessarily be a popular decision, but it has been made none-the-less."

Lucian nodded in approval. He had already seen several of his Thylacinians promoted to new ranks among Reivn's personal guard, and had realized he saw them as equals, not a lesser tribe.

Reivn caught his expression. *He approves. Good. I will need his help in the nights to come.* "Each of you already follow a Warlord, according to your location. I want to add to that. The portal system has not been largely used thus far for actual battle. Now, while it cannot be opened near Principatus troops, it can be used to transport fresh troops behind the lines to fortify positions and send reinforcements where they are needed. This will become a standard practice starting now. We can also use them to evacuate the wounded. It will save more lives. So, keep your Clerics at the ready during every battle."

From his place near the wall, Darius smiled. He liked Reivn's ideas so far. *I think we chose well, Lucian,* he telepathied the Thylacinian Warlord.

From across the room, Lucian shot him a look. *It would seem so. He's apparently been thinking through a great deal since we last saw him.*

Reivn looked around at the many faces and mixed reactions in the room. Some were angry. Others looked shocked. And some were showing obvious approval. "Our military units must become clearer and more concise. The loose way in which we have been structured creates confusion where not every warrior knows when or where they are needed. Not all of us live in barracks or stay in a specific location between battles. For those who wander, having an assigned unit to report to if called on would make gathering troops to defend a territory far easier. So I have begun implementing such a plan. Our people around the globe will be getting their assigned locations one at a time over the next few months. This does not mean they must live in these areas, but it does mean they must report to that area's assigned unit when summoned. The portals will make this easier to achieve. The Mastric tribe will become the conduit through which we can move our troops where they need to be in seconds. This will give us an advantage we have never before had."

Leshye listened intently as Reivn revealed his plans. She had long since believed they needed better structure in their fighting forces. Too often, when the call went out, only half as many as needed would show, and some of those only after the battle had already been lost. Arian had never really cared about trying to organize any tribes other than their own. She crossed her arms and leaned against the wall, her interest peaked. *Things are going to be a whole lot more interesting in the future,* she thought.

"I also want to implement a training schedule for each unit," Reivn continued, completely unaware of her thoughts. "While I realize most of our warriors are considered civilian volunteers by human standards, they do still need to know how to maximize their strengths and minimize their weaknesses. As I reassign people, I will be giving each unit a more balanced mix. As officers, you will need to learn how to utilize their strengths as a group. I witnessed first-hand how badly a battle can go, even with great leadership, when there is no organization. That problem is what cost us Djordji's life during the challenge. I have no desire to see this happen again. It was a needless death. You need to learn military tactics as our leaders. Those under you will follow commands, so it is your responsibility to lead them as successfully as you are able. The more you know of military battle strategies, the better you can defend your units should you get separated or cut off from the main group." He paused and looked around. "I know all of this is somewhat overwhelming for some of you, but I believe these changes will bring us more victories, while slowing down our losses. Every life has value, and squandering any of them needlessly under any circumstance will not be tolerated. I will no doubt be implementing further changes over time, but first, I need to better assess what happens among the ranks during battle. Are there any questions?"

With a grin, Leshye lifted her hand.

Reivn glanced her way and nodded. "Leshye... speak your mind."

"When do we start?" she asked with a twinkle in her eye.

Several people around the room laughed, as the atmosphere shifted to one of acceptance.

"Soon, Leshye," Reivn replied, keeping his composure in spite of the obvious change in the air.

From his position beside Reivn, Lunitar breathed a sigh of relief.

Reivn looked around, waiting to see if anyone else had any questions. When no one raised a hand, he finally nodded. "Yes... well, as no one else has anything to add, I believe my staff has prepared a banquet in the great hall. Please join me and enjoy all the hospitality Draegonstorm has to offer." Then he glanced at Lunitar. "Commander?"

Lunitar stepped forward. "Dragons, post!"

In one fluid motion, the contingent of extra Guards drew into a salute, crossing their rights fists over their chests before turning and marching out to return to their scheduled posts.

When they had gone, Reivn got up and made his way down the steps from the throne to join his officers.

Lunitar and Gideon followed, staying close to their father. Allies or not, they were not taking any chances.

Making his way over to Reivn, Lucian held out his hand and gave Reivn's a firm shake. "That was very well done, sir," he said enthusiastically. "And I greatly appreciate some of those changes you made to the ranks. I was tired of seeing my brethren misused. We put our lives on the line every night, but we are still treated as animals rather than equals. So, thank you."

Somewhat embarrassed by his candor, Reivn nodded. "Thank you, Lucian. I want to encourage change throughout our military and with any luck, eventually our society. I have never believed in the idea of lesser tribes or lesser people. We all stand shoulder to shoulder in battle, so we should stand shoulder to shoulder in peace."

"Well said, my lord," Alora purred as she approached. "Your words are wise. Let us hope others hear them." She slid her arm in his with a seductive smile, then stood on her toes to brush a kiss across his cheek. "I wanted to congratulate you on your promotion. It suits you." Then she leaned in and said, "Come to my room when it is all over and we will celebrate my way."

Reivn gazed down at her, his desire rising as he took note of the seductive gown she wore. "You look stunning tonight, my dear."

Behind Reivn, Lunitar stared at her in disapproval. He knew Reivn had invited her and her appearance now only served to concern him further. *Stay alert, Gideon. I still don't trust her.*

Gideon glanced at his brother and nodded silently.

Alora looked down at her neckline, which almost revealed too much bosom and then smiled at Reivn. "I had them make it for this occasion... just for you. I'll let you get back to your guests, but I'll be waiting for you..." She walked away, knowing many eyes were on her.

Lucian whistled. "Wow... where did you find her?"

"That is a story for another night," Reivn replied with a chuckle.

Leshye walked up then. "Congratulations, Reivn. I think you won them over. The talk in the room so far is almost all about the good you are bringing to this seat. There have been some complaints concerning the rank changes, but that is to be expected. Some of these sods do not understand the need for greater self-discipline. Personally, I like your ideas. I think they could well make a big difference in our losses overall."

Reivn frowned. "I am glad you think so. I have seen too many fall already, and we are nowhere close to a resolution or the end of this war. I actually wondered if I am moving too fast."

"No, you aren't," Darius chimed in, joining them. "You have the right as the Commander-in-Chief to make any change you wish as long as it is in keeping with the law and the Council's edicts. I think you chose well."

Accepting his handshake, Reivn hid his relief. So far, everything was going smoothly.

The banquet was a huge success, and by the end of it, most of the officers were toasting his new position and telling him how eager they were to work with him in the future. Lunitar and Gideon sat next to their father throughout the meal, but neither one said much. Both were busy noting who was who and silently taking names for later referencing.

When the meal concluded and guests began heading to either chambers to stay for the day or for the portal home, Reivn turned to his sons. "I am off. I have other business to see to. So I will bid you both a good day."

"May I assume by business, you mean your rendezvous with Alora?" Lunitar asked politely.

Reivn frowned. "What I do concerning her is my own business and does not involve you."

Lunitar nodded. "I understand that, father. I am only asking you to be careful. There is something about her that bothers me."

With a chuckle, Reivn patted his shoulder. "Perhaps it is because you have never met a Semerkhetian who did not embrace the Renegades before. She is a bit unusual. Now, I have somewhere to be. You both did well tonight. Get some rest." Without waiting for a response, he teleported away, leaving them standing in the middle of the banquet hall.

Gideon turned to stare at Lunitar. "He is being reckless," he pointed out. "Has he not seen how she is?"

"She is not like that around him, I guarantee it." Lunitar replied, his eyes showing his concern. "She no doubt puts on a show for him, and he is so taken with her, he does not see past it. Let us hope his infatuation will diminish soon."

Gideon did not reply. With a sigh, he simply walked away, heading toward his own chambers. He wanted to be alone.

Watching him go, Lunitar felt sorry for him. Events had moved so fast, Reivn had still not had time to talk to him and free him from thrall. So he had been left waiting. "Perhaps now that this affair is over with, he will see to Gideon's release, so we can all be at our best on the fighting field." There was no one but the servants in the room to hear him and after a moment's reflection, he finally turned and left.

Reivn knocked on Alora's door quietly.

"Come in, handsome," Alora purred from inside.

He walked in and was surprised to find her lounging on the bed in a silk garment that left very little to the imagination. The room was well-lit by candles and the bed turned down.

She patted a spot beside her. "I have waited all night for you, but you need not worry. I cast a waking spell in here. We will not sleep until we decide to."

He walked over and sat down beside her. "I had thought you did not want this between us. Have you changed your mind?"

"I have missed you too much, and realized I could not be without you anymore," she whispered, sitting up behind him to slide her arms over his shoulders and begin undressing him. "I crave your touch."

Reivn growled with desire and caught her hand, pulling her around and into his arms. "How could I not want you? You are such a bewitching creature."

She laughed and slipped her nightgown off, pulling him down to her neck. "You have no idea..."

## Chapter Fourteen
## Cruelty's Master

Valfort laid in the silence of a cold stone tomb where Mastric had bound him, his eyes closed as he tried to even his breathing. It had been weeks since his father had bound him and locked him away, refusing him sleep or nourishment, and forcing him to endure hours of confinement in the small space. He could hear the steady dripping of water as it ran down the damp walls of the catacombs and the occasional scurrying of rats as they moved about in the darkness, and it only served to remind him where he was. He tried to shut out the noise, but with no success. Opening his eyes again, he stared once more at the slab that sealed him in... mere inches from his face. "Father! Please let me out!" he screamed, knowing he was alone. "Father!"

Elena stood at the top of the stairwell, listening to him in silence. She was horrified he had been sealed inside a sarcophagus both awake and aware of his surroundings, and she worried that this time Mastric would break him. She had gone there every night to check on him. She had heard his screams and knew it would only end when Mastric wanted it to. "You were wrong to abandon Arian, brother, but you did not deserve this..." she whispered.

"Simple, sweet Elena... He deserved this and more," Mastric crooned as he appeared behind her. "His continued rebellion is a threat to our standing in the Council's chambers. My brethren already do not trust me. You know this. Do not pity the fool. I have punished him a thousand times and yet he still continues to disobey me. He does not represent our best interests when he continues to make enemies of those around us. He is alive. He should be thankful for that."

Elena gazed up at him, knowing what he was saying about the Council was true. However, another truth stood out too. He had changed over the centuries. His ever-increasing power had made him cold and unyielding, and now he often frightened her. She tried to plea with him on Valfort's behalf. "Beloved... he has been down there for weeks. Is it not time to release him and counsel him to use better judgement in future? He has been demoted, starved, and tortured for his foolish lack of judgement. However, he is still your son. I beg you... Please do not make him your enemy. I fear what would happen if he should turn on you."

Mastric reached up and stroked her cheek, making soft licentious, sucking noises. "I will consider it, but not now. My attention lies elsewhere. Come lay with me, my lovely."

Knowing she could not deny him, Elena nodded and leaned back into his arms, letting him wrap himself around her. Then she closed her eyes.

Within seconds they were in his lair, deep underground... far away from the Guild or any escape. His magic was the only way in... or out.

Mastric released her only long enough to rid her of her clothes. Then allowing himself to fully materialize, he morphed into a more youthful appearance before disrobing himself. He grabbed her and pulled her roughly against him, rubbing himself against her soft skin.

Elena surrendered to him, closing her eyes and allowing him to do what he wished. Her heart filled with sadness as she briefly remembered the man he had once been, and she allowed her mind and memory to carry her to a time when he was still gentle and kind, as he pushed her back on the bed.

With a hungry growl, he crawled across her like a ravenous animal and drove himself into her, as he lapped at her flesh. Then he pinned her arms above her and dove on her with a snarl, sinking his fangs into her throat and ripping it open to feast. His claws extended to a full six inches and drove into her arms, impaling them on the bed beneath her as he brutally laid claim to her. His skin turned hard and scaly as he moved, tearing the tender flesh between her thighs, but he ignored her pain and feasted on her, lapping at her blood like a child starving for milk.

Elena did not resist. Her body burned from the searing pain he inflicted on her, and the power he forced into her with every move made her body scream in agony, but she could only submit. She was his mate and had been since the day he created her. She had long since accepted this in him, and had created a place deep in herself where her mind could flee to escape the torture she now endured each time she laid with him. All remnants of his human compassion had long since evaporated with his physical form at the bottom of the Mystic Spirals.

When he was finished, he climbed off her. "You are still too weak. Your problem is that your compassion makes you foolish in your beliefs. We were born in darkness. If you embrace it wholly and allow the magic to consume you, pain is irrelevant and merely another physical experience. You still cling to human emotion and feeling as though you were a mere mortal. We are so much more than that. I am a God, and with the power I give you, you could peel the flesh from your bones and burn in the fires of the Spirals, and then wake the next evening to wrap yourself in their warmth. Nothing is impossible when you open your mind and allow yourself to experience everything. Why do you cling so to your mortality? This suffering benefits you nothing."

Elena laid where she was, trying to heal herself, but there was little strength left in her to do so. "I will try harder next time..." she whispered.

Mastric laughed. Then he sat back and watched her futile attempts at healing for several minutes while she endured the agony he had so savagely inflicted on her. Finally he said, "You cannot heal yourself without your blood. You know this. However, I can." He waved his hand over her. Every wound vanished, and her skin took on its normal, healthy glow. "That, my dear, is true unadulterated power." He grinned and ran his hand down the soft pale skin of her abdomen. "Such a magnificent gem of the night... my flawless alabaster pearl... you are perfection indeed."

Gazing up at him, she allowed her body to rest, knowing it would be many nights before he tired of her. "You have always seen me as such, beloved, but I still have much to learn yet." Her voice trembled in spite of her efforts to control it.

"I know. And I know you desire to learn more." Mastric grinned. "Do not worry. I have many things planned for you over the course of the next few nights, and we have nothing but time." He reached for her again and pulled her close. "However, first you need to feed. You must be in prime shape for our next round. I like it when your endurance is at its best."

Elena closed her eyes and gratefully accepted the warm fluid he offered, feeding from his neck as he wrapped his arms around her. She curled up to him, hoping for his gentle touch to return.

As she fed, he stood up, holding her in his arms. Then he pulled her legs around him and pinned them in an iron grip. He immediately shifted the flesh around his face and body, stretching it out to wrap around her upper torso, fusing her mouth against his neck and pinning her arms against him. Then he impaled her, shapeshifting his body to drive upwards and through her until he hovered just beneath her heart.

"You dare to think of that bastard in the catacombs and not me?" He snarled ferociously and stared into her frightened eyes. "Plea for him now, my sweet. I will end this for you if you can utter a single sound. Know that if you do, however, I will gut him slowly and hang him on a spit over Hellfire before taking his heart and feasting on it. Will you endure what suffering I give you to save him?" He laughed and raked his claws up her spine, ripping away the flesh to expose the raw nerves beneath. "Or will you succumb to your human side and beg for mercy, letting him die for your weakness?"

Tears poured down her cheeks and she trembled with the effort to keep from screaming as he ripped into her flesh and slowly skinned her while she was pinned helplessly against him. She shut her eyes tight, struggling to crawl back into her mind without success, but her silence was deafening.

"Irrelevance at its finest, Elena," he whispered in her ear. "Revel in the feel of depravity, knowing you can do anything if you but embrace the full flow of magic. Accept the pain. I can tear your body apart and rebuild it deep in the pool below. You would be reborn a Goddess." Shifting his face into a round and leechlike opening with hundreds of small razor sharp teeth protruding from around its edges, he bit down on her shoulder.

His bite caused searing white-hot pain as he shredded her flesh and crushed her bones. Then he tore the blood from her as fast as he gave it. "I will never stop tormenting you as long as you resist me. Like Valfort, you are mine. You live for my pleasure and will die should I so choose. So keep your silence and suffer." He laughed and grew spikes from the protrusion inside her, pushing them through her body to impale himself as well. Then he moaned with ecstasy, reveling in his depravity.

Elena finally lost consciousness, her body broken from the multitude of wounds.

Mastric felt her go limp and withdrew, reshaping himself into a man and releasing her. Then quickly healing the damage, he levitated her to the wall and suspended her there, wrapping her in invisible chains. Satisfied, he stretched out to stare at his favorite toy as he contemplated his jealousy over her concern for his son. Then with a cold smile, he closed his eyes and sent Valfort something to keep him company. When he was finished, he allowed himself to slip into slumber.

Down in the catacombs, Valfort's voice went unheeded as it echoed up the stairwell into the empty halls above. His brethren had returned to their own lairs, fleeing the Guild for fear of joining him in his punishment. So there was no one to hear his cries.

He stared at the stone slab above his face, fighting the claustrophobia that had set in. It was so close he could see every tiny line in the natural patterns that had formed over centuries in the ground before it was cut from a quarry. Shaking with the uncontrollable desire to beat against it until it broke, he yelled until he was hoarse.

Desperate to break the spell that held him in its iron grip, he began whispering his own. However, Mastric had taken that ability for now as well, and he knew he was no match for his father's magic. Mastric had ensnared him in a potent binding spell rendering him immobile, and his body would not obey him as long as Mastric held control. So, he could do nothing but lay there in the dark and weep, his remaining defenses collapsing and leaving him broken and enveloped with fear. He had been buried alive and did not know when or if his father would ever set him free again. He scraped his fingers against the stone beneath him in desperation until they bled, struggling to get his arms to move, but his efforts were in vain.

Then with a suddenness that startled him, he felt a jolt of magical energy shoot through him and wrap around his heart, encasing it in a shield. His eyes went wide with fear. He knew what it meant. It meant

Mastric had more planned for him. "No, no... please! Nothing else, Father! I'm begging you!"

Something moved beneath his hand, and he realized he was no longer alone. He began to panic. Then the first bite came, and he knew. Mastric had conjured flesh-eating beetles... just a handful. They would slowly eat him alive, and he would live through every second of it. His torture would be long and exceedingly brutal before his father would free him or heal him again. With his heart protected, he could not die. He would simply suffer until he longed for death... prayed for it even. And he would do so alone. As the beetles began to chew, he opened his mouth and screamed...

# THE BLOODLINE

## Chapter Fifteen
## Insanity's Descent

Mastric kept Elena in his lair for over a week, finding new ways to torment her as he tried to push her toward embracing her own oblivion in the depths beside him, but when she continued to resist his will, he finally tired of his games and teleported her back to the Guild above, depositing her unconscious body on her bed. Then he headed to his laboratory, where he had kept his newest protégé locked away for more than seven years.

Seth sat on his bed with his eyes closed, leaning against the lab wall. He had not seen the outside of his prison since Mastric captured him. That first year had been solely enduring Mastric's torture. Now he obeyed out of fear and studied hard. "Good evening, Master," he said, getting up when Mastric appeared. "Will we be working tonight?"

"No. I have other business." Mastric glided over to the table and sat down, looking expectantly at Seth. "First, however, I have decided it is time for you to grow. Get me a scroll."

Scurrying to tend him, Seth quickly handed him a scroll and quill, and then stood awaiting instructions.

Mastric stared at him. "Such willingness. My eldest son should take lessons from you on how to kiss one's boot." Then he laughed and got up. "You will do some reading tonight. I must visit Valfort to see if he has finally succumbed to my will, but first..." He held out his hand. "Give me your right arm."

Seth held out his arm nervously. "Have I done something wrong, master?"

"No. However, if you are to begin working for me, I must ensure you cannot go where you are not meant to." Mastric cut his wrist and bled him into a small cup. Then he dipped the quill into it and began scrawling sigils across the page.

The moment the first sigil was finished, Seth felt the magic rip through him with vicious efficiency as it began to burn its way into his spine. He dropped to his knees, screaming. The pain was excruciating. "Why?" He gasped for breath, the agony gripping every fiber of his being.

Mastric laughed. "I told you why. I own you, and as you will be working for me, I am ensuring you cannot run back to your insolent sire. With this, you will not only be unable to find him, you will not be able to avoid my summons."

Seth collapsed on the floor, curling into a ball as he struggled to shut out the pain.

"It will pass once the spell is complete," Mastric told him coldly. Then ignoring Seth completely, he got up and went to the bookshelves to retrieve a book. He dropped it on the table. "This should keep you occupied. I will return later."

The effects of the spell began to subside, and Seth got up shakily. He picked up the book and stared at the old leather cover. The pages between it glowed a brilliant green. "I will begin now, master," he whispered.

Mastric simply ignored him and disappeared.

Valfort was still in the tomb in the catacombs, but he had long since fallen silent, most of his throat eaten away. Part of his face hung half off, and sections of his body were almost down to the bone. He had succumbed to a sort of madness and laid there, no longer caring about anything but his need to feed. His hunger had grown insatiable, his body having thinned and grown gaunt from lack of sustenance. In desperation, he had gnawed at the parts of his lips he could suck into his mouth, chewing on them to get at his own blood until they were ragged and torn beyond further reach.

A black mist formed beside the sarcophagus, and Mastric stepped from its depth. He stared down at the tomb in silence, contemplating whether he would open it. Finally, he waved his hand and the heavy stone slab floated sideways where it settled to rest against the stone base.

Opening his one remaining eye, Valfort did not realize he was not hallucinating at first. His father's face loomed above him. He blinked again to be sure. Then he opened his mouth, but he could not speak.

Mastric banished the beetles back to oblivion. Then he healed Valfort's neck and head alone, so he could talk again.

Feeling his vocal cords and throat reform, Valfort gasped and began to beg, "Please, father! I swear to you I will not fail you again. Please... let me out of here! Please no more!" He started to sob, fear of once more being locked away reducing him to a broken and miserable child. "I swear I'll obey... I swear."

Lifting him from the sarcophagus, Mastric pulled him close. "Then feed. You must regain your strength."

Valfort shakily bit into Mastric's neck, starving for blood.

Mastric allowed him to drink his fill and patiently waited until he withdrew.

It did not escape Valfort's notice. He had taken far more than Mastric should have had in his entire body. He pulled back, slightly gorged and trembling from the power surging through him. "Th... thank you, father." Searing pain began to shoot through his body as the reformation began and he looked up, hoping his father would heal him.

Mastric had other plans. In one swift motion, he extended a claw and decapitated him. Then holding Valfort's head with one hand, he cauterized both sides and dropped his body back into the sarcophagus.

Valfort's eyes went wide with panic. He knew as long as Mastric kept his heart intact, he could do almost anything to him without killing him, and the thought terrified him.

Mastric smiled and stared into his frightened eyes. "You will decorate my laboratory wall until your body heals of its own accord. Perhaps by then, you will learn the obedience you promised me. This is your final opportunity to convince me of your loyalty. I did consider simply leaving you in that damp grave to rot." He sealed the sarcophagus with a whisper and then teleported to his lab, taking Valfort's head with him.

*Father...* Valfort telepathied. *...mercy... please!*

With a cold laugh, Mastric gazed at him. "I gave you mercy. You are alive, and now, we have much to discuss about your future."

Broken now, tears fell down Valfort's face. He had no idea what Mastric had planned, but it no longer mattered. He would be a puppet until his master tired of him. He opened his mouth to scream, but no sound would come.

For the next two months, Valfort's head adorned the wall of Mastric's lab while his body slowly healed and regrew in the catacombs. Mastric would often completely ignore his suffering, and at times even revel in it. However, he would occasionally stop to taunt him over his failures. It did not matter to Valfort, who could no longer see beyond the desperate need to be reunited with his body.

The night finally arrived when Mastric pulled him down from the wall. He gazed at Valfort's face from beneath his hood, before lowering it to reveal the empty space beneath. "You have forgotten what I am, for it can be the only explanation as to why you grew so arrogant. Either that, or you have grown so foolish you are no longer worth the effort to keep you alive."

Panic rising in him, Valfort could only stare at the void in front of him, knowing the truth of his father's existence.

Mastric held him in silence for a long time, pondering over what to do with him. Finally he said, "It is fortunate for you that I do not believe in wasting any resource, no matter how insignificant. Come. Your body is ready for your head." In an instant, he had teleported them both to the catacombs. Then opening the sarcophagus with a mere thought, he aligned Valfort's head and neck, and then fused them back together.

Valfort gasped at the pain that tore through his entire being when his nerves, muscles and bones reconnected again, and he found his voice, letting out a scream of agony.

Smiling in satisfaction, Mastric left him lying there. "When you can get up, you may come back upstairs," he stated and then disappeared.

Valfort laid there for a long time, letting his body heal, until he could finally grab the edge of the tomb and pulled himself up. More than a little shaken by the events of the last few months, he slowly climbed out of the sarcophagus, falling to the floor beside it. His body felt weak and unwilling to hold him up, and his newly repaired muscles were still having difficulty remembering how they worked. So, he struggled like a child as he got to his feet and staggered toward the stairs.

Elena was just coming to check on him and heard him. She rushed down the stairs to his aid. "Brother! You are free! Here, let me help you." She touched him gently on the shoulder and began pouring her healing energy into him, finishing the job Mastric had left for him to do.

He flinched at her touch, feeling the raw power pouring from her fingertips. But then the pain started to ease and he slowly relaxed, letting her repair the damages. It was not the first time she had healed him after one of Mastric's punishments. ...*but it will be the last,* he promised himself.

After a few tense minutes, she stepped back. "There. Your wounds are almost completely healed."

Looking down at his body, he frowned. "You've gained more power again. It has obviously been beneficial having so much favor with father."

"Ceros, please don't be like that. You have no idea what it's like. Just like you, I endure what I must to survive." Elena fell silent, afraid to say any more for fear Mastric was still listening.

However, Valfort was angry and did not care. "You have always found favor with him... you and Reivn both! No doubt, Reivn has been trying to usurp my position while I was in there!"

Elena shook her head, realizing he still did not know what had happened in his absence. "Ceros... you have no position. You were demoted, have no seat on the Council, and are not even listed in the Guild Guards right now. Mastric has not yet reassigned you, and probably will not as long as you behave this way."

Valfort snarled at her. "He will reinstate me as Warlord now that I am done my punishment! He always does! But I know Reivn! He was no doubt trying to garner favor from father in my absence! When I am reinstated, I will deal with him!"

Worried now, Elena reached out and caught his arm. "Ceros, you aren't going to be reinstated. Reivn is our Warlord now. Father also took him before the Council as a candidate for the position of Commander-in-Chief. He found favor among the other Warlords and was awarded the position after the challenge was complete. He is the new Commander-in-Chief for the Alliance, brother. You cannot touch him and expect to live. Father will never allow it."

"So what am I supposed to do?" Valfort growled, suddenly feeling very insecure about his own future. "He has taken everything from me! He did this deliberately because I was not there to stop him!" His rage slowly building, he pushed Elena's hand away. "He has always been jealous of my status and used this as his opportunity to steal my prestige and title!"

Elena stepped back, stunned by the bitterness in his voice. "Reivn has never wished you ill, Ceros. He's too kind-hearted and honorable for that. You know as well as I do that father would not have given him a choice. In this family, Mastric alone decides what we do and where our fate lies. You know this better than anyone as the oldest of us."

With a snarl, Valfort slapped her across the face. "You have always defended him! One might wonder where your true loyalty lies... with father or your precious brother!"

Holding her cheek, Elena stared at him in shock. "Ceros... what are you saying? I am loyal to all our family, including you! Reivn is your brother! You should not speak so ill of him."

Valfort turned to face her, and a cold hatred filled his eyes. "That Sarmatian filth is no brother of mine. He is as beneath me as you. Go back to your master, Elena! There is nothing more you can do here." Without another word, he limped up the steps.

"Ceros wait!" Elena called after a moment. She scrambled up the steps after him, but he had already disappeared.

When Valfort reappeared in his room, he began to pace, his fury over Reivn's appointment growing, and with it, his bitterness. "How dare he! He was a slave! I was a general... a God among men! He cannot replace me! He will never be my equal, and I refuse to serve under him! I cannot believe father would shame me this way! He has betrayed me! They all have!" He slowly worked himself into a frenzy, his hatred cemented as he thought of Reivn's promotion. After hours of pacing, his thoughts finally turned another direction, and after long minutes of contemplation, he made up his mind. Now he just needed to find a way to put his plan into action. A new glint in his eyes, he settled down just as the dawn began to cross the horizon.

# THE BLOODLINE

## Chapter Sixteen
## Aeternal Pact

Reivn awoke next to Alora and turned to stare at her. He had been with her every night for almost a month now and had spent much of his waking hours in her company.

"You're awake," Alora purred, rolling over and curling into his arms. "I had thought you would be asleep for at least another hour." She trailed her fingers down his chest, teasing him as she climbed on top of him. "I'm hungry, beloved."

He smiled and wrapped his arms around her. "I can send for a servant if you would like."

She shook her head and inhaled his scent deeply. "No... I have fed on the servants enough. I have a taste for you."

He gazed at her in astonishment. "A bond? I have wanted to do so with you for some time, but I did not think you wished it, so I have not asked." He offered her his wrist.

She laughed and pushed it away. "Oh, no, my love. This is much better." She crawled upward until she was right above him, and then leaned down and sank her fangs into his throat. Then she moaned with pleasure as she drank from him.

Surprised, he briefly hesitated before wrapping his arms around her again and pulling her closer. He winced slightly at her ferocity but allowed her to continue.

Finally, she drew back and licked her lips, purring like a cat. "That was by far more satisfying than I imagined. Now... your turn." She slipped her gown off and laid back down on top of him naked, tilting her head and inviting him to feed.

Stirring from his reverie, he growled hungrily and pulled her closer, biting into her neck gently so he would not injure her. A light-headed ecstasy poured through him as they melded their blood together, and he closed his eyes, enjoying the pure sensations that filled every fiber of his being. When he finished, he carefully licked her wound and closed it before letting her go.

She closed her eyes, reveling in the forming bond and searching his blood for whatever secrets it held. She found something interesting. "Reivn, my love, you never stop pleasing me. This feels so... warm... like a good fur on a cold night. However, I am confused about one thing. Why did you not tell me you were Dragonborn?"

"What?" He stared up at her in surprise. "What do you mean? I am Sarmatian by birth and Mastric by blood."

Alora smiled and sat up, changing position to ease herself down on top of him. Then she began to slowly ride him, teasing his sexuality as she spoke. "You, my love, are not just a Sarmatian, or even just human turned Vampyre for that matter. You are only half human... or at least you were before Mastric claimed you. Your blood does not lie. Did you not know?"

Reivn fell silent as he sifted through his memories of the past, trying to see any connection to what she was saying, but he could not think of a single time when it had ever been mentioned. "I think you must be mistaken, Alora. My parents were both from the same tribe I was raised in, and I had many years with them before they passed. There was never any mention of such things and everything I was taught was that which our tribal ancestors passed down to each generation in turn. I was bred to be a warrior from the time I could walk. Indeed, Dragons were nothing more than the symbols we bore on our shields."

At his statement, she laughed. Then she wiggled a bit, enticing him to taste of her favors again.

He lost all thought of anything but her, and with a growl, rolled her onto her back and pinned her to the bed. "Tell me, my wicked little enchantress... what makes you even think I am a Dragonborn?" he whispered in her ear, moving in and out of her and teasing her as he spoke, building the tension between them.

"It was in your blood. I can taste it. All Semerkhetians have that skill. It's part of our birthright," she moaned, reveling in their play. Then she clawed at his back and rose to meet him, not wanting him to pry any further into her abilities.

He lost all control and the discussion ended abruptly, as he began making love to her in earnest, all thoughts of their conversation gone.

Allowing the tide of passion to carry her away, she submersed herself in her lust and focused only on his attentions.

Hours later, Reivn laid holding her in his arms, staring at the ceiling.

"Beloved?" Alora ventured softly, breaking the silence. "Marry me."

He stirred from his thoughts and turned to gaze at her. "Hmm... what did you say?"

She smiled up at him and began trailing her fingers through his long hair. As she spoke, she invoked the blood she had drunk from him and began to manipulate it. Her eyes turned a soft gold and she met his gaze with a new potency he was unfamiliar with and indeed, did not even notice. "I said I want to marry you."

He pulled away and stared down at her in confusion, her hypnotic effect clouding his mind like a heavy drug. "You are serious."

She laughed. "You know me well enough to understand I would not ask if I was not. So?"

"What of your vow?" He struggled to shake the fog off that veiled his mind, making clear thought almost impossible. However, the more he gazed at her, the more the thought filled his mind that she was the key to the happiness he had been seeking for centuries.

Knowing she had already won, Alora kissed him, her eyes still interlocked with his and weaving their magic over him beyond any point of return. Then she sat up, draped her legs over the side of the bed, and pulled on a robe before getting up. "Things have changed, beloved. I want to stay at your side. Being away from you now would be... painful. Do you no longer desire me?"

His mind thoroughly confused now, Reivn smiled at the thought of having such a beauty as his bride, and the endless nights of pleasure that would lie ahead. He got up and walked over to wrap his arms around her. "I desire you more than ever, my beautiful Egyptian Queen. You haunt my dreams and fill my mind with intoxicating thoughts every waking hour. You have made a slave of me, I think." He paused, as he fought for clarity of thought. "Now, knowing my father may have lied to me about the truth of my existence, I feel more alone than ever. Having you by my side would bring me great joy."

She smiled and turned in his arms to face him. He was hers. "I had not thought of that," she lied. "If Mastric did hide this from you, how will you ever discover the truth of it?"

"I intend to confront him with this new information, but before I do, I think we should see to our marriage. Then I can petition the Council concerning your acceptance into the Alliance, which would also place you under their protection. That way, he cannot attack you or refute your claim in my life. You would have the safety of being the Commander-in-Chief's wife. So, how soon do you want to marry?" He gazed down into her dark eyes in sincerity, wanting to please her. Even though the fog was lifting, the course was set in his mind.

She shrugged and pulled away. "I do not need a grand wedding ceremony to be happy with you. All we need is a priest to make it official. Perhaps we can discover more concerning your past at the same time. You must have at least some facts to bring to the table when you discuss this with Mastric." Walking to the wardrobe, she pulled out clothing for both of them. "If we hurry and bathe, we can slip away to begin our search before anyone even notices. I know a number of holy men who could see to our marriage while we are away, if it is truly what you want."

Completely mesmerized, his eyes followed her every move. "It is," he answered without a second thought. "I think I have fallen in love with you. I want you more than you know and even more than I realized. And now that I know about this... other side of me, I must learn all I can before I speak with Mastric. I must know the truth."

"Then let us go to the baths and be away." She handed him his clothes, caught him by the hand and slipped out the door with him.

Reivn and Alora were gone for weeks before they returned to Draegonstorm, and when they stepped through the portal, it was obvious to everyone that something had drastically changed.

Reivn had not said anything to anyone before slipping away, and concern over his whereabouts had Lunitar vigilantly watching for him and awaiting his return. So the moment the portal opened, he felt it and looked up from his book. *He is finally back.* He quickly teleported to the portal chamber, expecting to greet his father. He was surprised to find no one there. "Did his lordship just come through?" he asked the Guard on duty.

The guard shook his head. "No, my lord. The portal has remained silent all night."

Disturbed, Lunitar headed for Reivn's laboratory immediately, knowing he had a small portal there as well. *It was definitely him I felt...* he thought to himself as he raced through the halls.

Reivn was just opening the door to his lab when Lunitar arrived. He looked up and smiled. "Lunitar... good! We have much to discuss. Meet me in the Commonroom in a few minutes. I must see to new quarters for Alora first."

His concern growing as he looked past Reivn and saw who was with him, Lunitar looked from one to the other. Then he slowly nodded, trying to figure out what was happening. "Of course, and welcome home my lord."

Alora sashayed past him with a grin. "Lunitar, how are you?"

"I am fine, my lady. Thank you for asking." Lunitar answered, trying not to show his irritation. Then he turned to Reivn. "You have been missed these past few weeks, my lord. However, all is in order and has gone according to plan for the reorganization of the Guard."

Holding out his hand to Alora, Reivn nodded, pleased at the obvious progress. "Excellent, Commander. I will escort her to her quarters and then join you. I will not be long."

Lunitar bowed. "Then by your leave, my lord." Reivn and Alora vanished, leaving Lunitar standing there in stunned silence for second before making his way to the Commonroom. When he got there, he summoned a sound shield and blanketed the entire room. Then he stood staring at the fire in silence, hands clasped behind his back as he waited.

Gideon hurried in seconds later. "Am I late?" he quickly asked. "Father sent me a summons."

"No, you're not late... or maybe you are. It's hard to tell." Lunitar replied quietly. "I think we both may be too late."

The door closing behind them caught their attention as Reivn walked in. "You are neither one late. Please... sit down. We have much to discuss." He walked over to join them.

His expression one of confusion, Gideon seated himself on the sofa, wondering what this was about.

Lunitar turned and leaned against the mantle with one elbow. "If you don't mind, father. I think I want to be on my feet for this one."

Reivn raised an eyebrow and looked from one to the other of them. "You need not be so serious. I have not ended the world, I promise you. I want to begin this conversation by telling you both I have taken a bride. Alora is the new Lady of Draegonstorm."

Gideon half-got up from his seat. "You... she... What?"

Lunitar nodded to himself, realizing this was a serious problem. "I am happy for you, father," he stated carefully, arching his eyebrow. Inside, he did not feel nearly as calm. His mind was racing ahead to the possibilities.

Gideon stared at Reivn open-mouthed in shock. "But father... she is a Semerkhetian! Won't the Council have a problem with you allying yourself with a potential Renegade?"

"She has sworn allegiance to the Council and was accepted as my wife last night," Reivn replied. "So no, it will not be a problem. She has full rights under the law and the protection of this house."

Closing his eyes for a moment as his news sank in, Lunitar sighed. "Then we must as the very least acknowledge this momentous event with a feast," he stated, noting his father's mood. "The court will need to be introduced to the wife of the Prince."

Reivn glanced over at Lunitar shrewdly. "You do not approve of my union," he observed. "Is it because of her tribe?"

Lunitar shook his head. "No. It is all just very new to me, father. It will take some time to adjust. A month ago, you were not even thinking about marriage and now you are married. This was just very sudden, so I need some time to get used to the idea. Please forgive me."

"It is I who should be asking for forgiveness. I should have told you before I left, but for some reason, it just seemed right to keep it to ourselves until we returned." Reivn looked confused for a moment, as though searching for the right words. "I have been a bit preoccupied by her these last few weeks, and our happiness has been almost surreal. I suppose I just wanted to enjoy the moment while it was there. It has been so long..." His voice trailed off into silence.

Gideon stared at his father in concern before glancing up at his brother, his eyes speaking volumes.

Lunitar shook his head slightly, indicating they needed to stay quiet for now.

Reivn did not notice the interchange and seemed as though he was trying to sort something out in his own head. Then he shook himself and looked up. "I am sorry. What were we speaking of?"

"Plans for a feast to introduce Alora to the Court," Lunitar answered. He had not missed how uncharacteristically distracted Reivn was and it greatly concerned him.

With a brief nod, Reivn got up and walked over to Lunitar. Then patting him on the shoulder, he smiled. "An excellent idea. I will let you handle the plans for that."

Lunitar bowed his head to avoid making eye contact. "Thank you, father."

"Now on to other matters," Reivn stated. "I will be going to Mastric's Guild tomorrow. I must speak with him on a matter of great importance, and it will not keep. I need answers and only he can tell me what I want to know."

Gideon got up then. "Um, are we missing something? You want to talk to Mastric? Whatever for?"

"Father has his reasons, and we have much to plan," Lunitar interjected, not wanting Gideon to get himself into trouble. "Come Gideon. Give me a hand."

Reivn frowned, wondering why Lunitar was being so elusive. "Are you not feeling well, my son?" he asked, catching Lunitar's arm.

Lunitar looked up. "No, father. I feel fine. However, we have an event to plan for, and you have a trying conversation ahead of you for whatever you are pursuing with Mastric." He paused before adding, "I am merely seeking to carry some of the weight here to give you time to enjoy your newly acquired nuptials."

With a frown, Reivn let him go. "Then I will let you do what you must," he said somewhat stiffly. "I will be in the library for the remainder of the evening doing research for tomorrow."

Gideon looked uncomfortably from one to the other before saying "Congratulations again, father," and slipping from the room.

Following him out, Lunitar remained silent. He knew a dismissal when he heard one.

Reivn watched them go, unaware of exactly how much Alora had just driven a wedge between he and his sons or how much things were about to change.

## Chapter Seventeen
## Manipulated Blood

"Father, I must speak with you!" Reivn yelled as he walked into the Mastric's Senate chamber.

Mastric materialized on his throne, and his eyes narrowed as he stared at his son. "Lower your voice, boy! You are squealing like a mouse at the moment of its death! What is it you want?"

Reivn walked over and knelt before him, putting his hand over his chest in salute. "My lord, I have questions I must be allowed to ask. Please... I need to know."

"Get up and ask your questions then," Mastric rumbled, annoyed at the intrusion. "You are a Commander-in-Chief. You do not kneel... even to me. Your brethren must see you as second only to me in our tribe."

Realizing it would only help his cause, Reivn immediately got up, and then bowed respectfully to his father before continuing. "I will remember that in the future, my lord."

Eyeing him in curiosity, Mastric waved Reivn over to sit with him. "You seem troubled. What could possibly have happened to garner your concern so soon? You have not held your position long enough to have felt its burdens as of yet. So what then?"

Reivn took a seat across from him, hesitating for a moment before explaining. "I came here because I discovered something about myself that I was previously unaware of. You are omnipotent in all ways, so I assume you knew about it and chose for some reason not to enlighten me. Now I have discovered it on my own and hope you will tell me why. I want to know more about it, and also why it was kept from me."

Mastric leaned back in his seat. "That is quite a build-up. This is obviously important to you, so continue."

"I recently discovered I am a Dragonborn, and in fact was never human at all," Reivn blurted out, unable to contain himself. "Knowing you as I do, I realized you had to have known this long ago. I am curious as to the nature of my beginnings and heritage. I have as of yet not uncovered those origins. Please, father. How did this come to be and why did you not tell me?"

Stirring in his seat, Mastric sniffed the air and then growled dangerously. "You have the stench of foreign magic all over you, Reivn. What have you done to yourself?" He opened his eyes to the plains of the Spirals and gazed through them, frowning when he saw the aura rising from his son.

However, Reivn was persistent and would not be deterred. "Father, I beg you, do not ignore me this time. I truly need to know. Were my parents even my parents? Is everything I remember a lie?"

"No, it is not a lie," Mastric stated impatiently. "Your parents and their parents and the people before them were all part of your noble lineage, and yes, you are descended from the Dragons who once roamed these lands. They returned to Ban Drui long ago, and only a scattered few remained behind. Your ancestor was one of them."

Reivn stared at Mastric in shock. "You knew about it all this time and never told me? Why?"

Mastric stared at him, his eyes cold and uncaring. "Would it have made any difference in who you are?" he asked bluntly. "Would it have granted you some divine knowledge into the arcane?"

"No, but it is a part of me, and that knowledge could have led me to seek out knowledge from my own kind that could be useful in this war." Reivn was angry and felt betrayed.

Unconvinced, Mastric was not finished. "This magic on you... it is Semerkhetian. Perhaps it is you who should explain yourself better."

"I married two weeks ago," Reivn replied. "My wife is both accepted by the Council and a member of the Alliance, but she is in fact a Semerkhetian by blood. It is no doubt she you smell on me."

His visage darkening considerably, Mastric snarled at him. "You took a wife without my consent? And one from an unaccepted tribe? Have you lost your senses entirely? Have you forgotten I hold your son as a prisoner here?"

"No, father. I have not forgotten," Reivn growled in frustration. "I do everything you ask and serve as I always have... loyally!"

Mastric tapped his finger impatiently on the arm of his throne. "You forget that even a Warlord can fall from grace. I put you where you are now. Do not disappoint me. We have much to do in the nights ahead. I have plans for you, and you will not destroy them over some foolish whim. I will allow no woman, no child... nothing to get in the way of your work."

Reivn glared at him. "I wanted some happiness for myself and she gives me that!"

"She is a Semerkhetian! I have half a mind to destroy her just for your allowing her to taint you in such a fowl way! Her magic clings to you like the fungus on the catacomb walls. It covers you with the smell of foul, unholy things. You will end up regretting this alliance with her, Reivn. Mark me on that," Mastric warned him. "You play now with things you do not truly understand. A snake is always a snake, no matter how beautiful its skin."

Losing his patience, Reivn got up. "She is not evil! She does not participate in the rites so many of her tribe's people do. She has actually been helping me these past few weeks to search for any knowledge we could find about my own lineage. So enough about her, father... please! I came to learn the truth about myself and my past."

At that, Mastric laughed. "Your tone has certainly grown quite bold of late. Is this your new face, Warlord? Watch your tongue with me or I'll cut it out for you! You want to know about your past? Very well. Then I shall tell you. I am actually surprised it took you this long to uncover it, considering you turned Lunitar and felt his turning so intimately. You do not understand any of this yet, do you? I sent you to collect him. I arranged for you to attack the village while he was away, knowing you in your infinite mercy would bring him back to save just one of the many lives you claimed that night. I kept him all those years waiting for the time when you would ask for him. I allowed you to turn him because I wanted you to. I even collected your son Gideon when you thought to leave him behind to die in Rome, made him a blood servant and preserved him for over a thousand years just to give him to you when the time was right. Had you not turned Seth, I might have even held on to him a while longer. However, you forced my hand. Now, you are all of the same bloodline. Did you really think any of this a coincidence? I have never taken you for a fool before, Reivn. Open your eyes! You already know the answers to your questions, you just do not wish to accept them."

Reivn fell silent, his thoughts racing as he considered all the events of his past and Lunitar's with Mastric, and after several minutes of contemplative thought, his eyes widened, and he looked at his father in disgust. "Because Gideon is my son by birth, you wanted him as insurance to make certain my bloodline's continuation was safe through him. But why Lunitar? He was not born of my family and is not of my blood. So how does he fit into this? Why was it so important I bring him back from that mission? Why did you want him so badly?"

Mastric got up and glided to the door. "The answer lies at your fingertips, Reivn. Search your soul. He is indeed of your blood. You felt it the moment you turned him. It is why you were drawn to him even before you turned him and why I had you kill an entire village to obtain him. Like you, he is a valuable asset because he is likewise... a Dragonborn." He vanished into the black mist, leaving Reivn to stare after him in shock.

Reivn dropped back into his seat, the truth sinking into him with terrible finality. Not one moment of his Immortal existence had been an accident. Mastric had known from the first time he had seen him exactly what he was and had been grooming him for some unknown purpose from the start. "Dear God... How can I ever tell Lunitar any of this? The raid...

the death toll... the countless years of slavery and suffering... Mastric planned it all, and like a blind fool, I followed him. I was the sword he wielded to take what he wanted. I was such a simpleton... believing him capable of mercy. Lunitar lived because it was his plan all along, and I delivered him into the hands of his tormentor and mine." Dropping his head in his hands, he covered his face, horrified that he had been fooled into taking not just another life, but one of his own kind, and condemning them to the same fate as he himself had fallen into. "God help me... what have I done?"

## Chapter Eighteen
## The Bloodline

Reivn summoned Lunitar to his office the moment he returned to Draegonstorm. Then he began pacing the room in agitation. He did not have long to wait.

"You sent for me, father?" Lunitar poked his head in, and seeing Reivn's anxious state, wondered what had happened.

Reivn turned to gaze at him with troubled eyes. *I cannot even explain it to him. I barely understand it myself. What am I supposed to tell him?* Keeping an even expression, he nodded. "I did. We must talk. We have plans to make."

Lunitar walked over and sat down. The he waited, looking up at Reivn expectantly.

"We must be frank with each other as we once were," Reivn began, as he searched for the right words. "I fear the events of the last two months have put us at odds, and at this time, we simply cannot afford that. We must be one unified front. I have entered a position where Mastric can no longer touch me without due cause, and I believe we need to ensure this remains the case. I never again want him to meddle in our affairs. I no longer trust him." Reivn paused, wondering how to explain his last statement.

Concern crossing his features, Lunitar gazed up at him. "That may be the case for you, father, but he can still meddle with the rest of us. So we must tread carefully."

Reivn growled. "Not as long as you command my personal Guard. That makes you answerable only to me."

"Perhaps," Lunitar replied. "...but what of Gideon... or Alora?" he added as an afterthought.

"I will make Gideon my personal escort," Reivn stated after thinking for a second. "And Alora is my wife and an accepted member of the Alliance now. So she is afforded full protection under the law. Because she is not a Mastric, he also has no say on her behalf. So that should solve any potential issues. However, we must use caution. There is much about him you do not know. I had not realized before just how inhuman he truly is."

Lunitar raised an eyebrow, somewhat surprised by Reivn's vehemence and bitterness toward Mastric, and he grew worried, as it was quite uncharacteristic for him. "What have you discovered, father. It is no trifling thing that would easily break your loyalty to anyone."

Reivn turned to stare at his son, and for one brief second, he almost broke and told him. Then he stopped himself and said. "We have seen how cruel he is to Valfort and others, Lunitar, and we are now in his sights. He craves power and through us, or more specifically me, he would claim enough power that he could destroy the Alliance if he chose... and I firmly believe given the opportunity, he would do so."

"Well, father, know that as always, I am loyal to you," Lunitar replied, wanting to reassure him. "...for it is you who saved me from becoming a monster far worse than humans think us."

Turning away so Lunitar would not see the guilt he felt so keenly, Reivn stared at the fire. "I have been blindly loyal to my own father for far too many years. I do not want that kind of loyalty from you. Should I ever stray from my own honor and the honor of this house, I expect you to call me on it. I can ask no less from you."

Lunitar stirred uncomfortably in his seat before replying. "With that being said, father... you have trained me to kill Martulians and Semerkhetians on sight. Yet not only did you bring one into this house, but you brought it into our family by marrying it."

Reivn turned around, a surprised look on his face. "I thought you understood that although we do kill the Martulians and Semerkhetians, I have always held that innocence is innocence. This includes the senseless killing of anyone who has done no wrong. Has she in some way offended or attacked you? Has she broken our laws?"

"She has not harmed me in any way, and no... she has not broken any laws." Lunitar sighed. "...but she has taken a man I have known for centuries to be reserved and thoughtful and completely unhinged him. You married her inside of two months of knowing her, and I'm assuming have bonded with her, after centuries of no interest in romantic interludes. With just that alone, even if she were from one of the Alliance tribes, it would have raised my suspicions. However, she is from the one tribe that is most notorious for manipulation. So, yes! I am distrustful of her and her motives. I hope you love her, and perhaps in time, I will grow to not be suspicious of her. There is more going on here than I know. If nothing else, you have taught me to trust my instincts, and my instincts tell me something is very wrong. I am sorry for my harsh candor."

Reivn stood silent for a moment, absorbing what he said. Finally, he nodded. "I do see every point you have made as being a valid concern, and I will take it under serious advisement. However, I ask you to remember there are wheels within wheels turning at the helm that guides this family, and all of us, myself included, must strive with each and every moment we are alive, to ride out the storms and revel in what small kindnesses we can. They will be far fewer from here on in."

"I will strive to do so father. Know that I will keep an open mind and not look for fault, but I will also not overlook fault. I swore to stand by you and protect you, and I will do so no matter who threatens you."

"That is why I summoned you and not your brother. There are things I am not prepared to discuss at this time. However, you must know that our bloodline stands on its own now, and we must raise it up to become a power that is not only respected but feared among all the tribes. That is how we survive."

"Then we have a lot of work to do..."

## Epilogue

Valfort stood in the shadows impatiently watching the few people who
passed by him. It had taken him weeks to find anyone who would believe
him enough to set him up with a connection who could help him. Now he
worried the man would not show.

After about twenty minutes, a fellow dressed in dark clothing came up
the street, hugging the walls and remaining as invisible to passersby as
possible.

*That has to be him,* Valfort thought to himself. As had been arranged,
he stepped under the streetlamp momentarily, so his red cloak would be
visible. Then he moved back into the shadows to await his contact.

The man saw him and slowly crossed the street, looking back over his
shoulder to be sure he was not followed. Then he turned down the alley
near where Valfort was waiting.

Valfort watched him in relief. *There's the signal,* he thought and took
his cue, waiting about five minutes before following. He made sure no one
saw him and hurried into the alley, looking for the man who was supposed
to be meeting him.

Without warning, someone grabbed Valfort from behind and put a
knife to his throat. "Do what I say and not a word. Now put your hands
where I can see them and walk."

Valfort held his hands clearly in front of him and started walking. He
knew he could easily use his magic and kill his attacker, but he was not
willing to risk losing his only chance to make contact. It had taken him
weeks just to get this far.

The man guided him to the end of the alleyway and an old wood door
that led to an extremely run down shack, and then pushed him inside. Only
then did he let Valfort go. "You the fool Mastric saying he wants to meet
my master?" he asked.

Brushing himself off in disgust, Valfort turned around. "I am. My
name is..."

"Your name don't matter any!" His host was uneasy and shifted
nervously. "How do I know you ain't trying to set me up or use me as
bait?" The man eyed him with suspicion. 'I hear you been asking questions
all 'round London. I know your tribe. None of you leave and tell about it.
So how do I know I can trust you?"

Valfort sighed and shook his head in irritation. "It is true not many
Mastrics make it out. That is because Mastric kills them if he so much as
suspects they are doing any less than his bidding. I have spent weeks
developing a spell that shields my movements long enough that I actually

could talk to someone. I want out, and I want it badly enough I'm willing to share some of my arcane knowledge with your hierarchy."

The man broke into raucous laughter. "My boss? He isn't nobody who could do magic! He barely survived his six months! He don't have no rank and just does what he's told... like me! You think you going to give him magic? What a gaffe!"

Growing annoyed with his tone, Valfort had enough and hit him with a binding spell.

"Here now! What do you think you are you doing? Who are you?" his host exclaimed, growing fearful.

Valfort moved closer to him and growled. "I am a Mastrics Elder who wants guaranteed help in leaving. Do you understand that, you stinking pig-sucking toad?" He grabbed the man's chin and got in his face. "I know your sire cannot do magic. None of you insects can! He probably doesn't even bathe himself! My gift is not meant for him! It is meant for the master of his masters!"

The man turned pasty white, realizing how powerful Valfort was and that he was no match for the magic levied against him. "I'll tell him about you, no worries! Let me off, will you? I was just doing my job!"

Sniffing the air directly in front of him, Valfort pulled back in disgust. "My God, you stink! I will never get that stench out of my cloak. I'll have to burn it..." He paused, as an idea suddenly came to him, and putting on a smile, he turned around. "...unless you would like it as a gift of good will... a show of faith?"

"You would give me that?" The man stared at him in awe. "It's mighty fine, it is. I don't have a cloak..."

Valfort grinned. Now he was getting somewhere. "Then you take my message to your master and tell him what I said. This has to be done carefully or I will lose my life before I can get free."

The man thought about it and then nodded. "It will take a while to find my master. We don't go with ours like you. We have to find what we can to get by. I do my job and report to those who come looking for me. So I have to wait until they send someone."

"I can wait. I will bring you other things you can either sell or use, as long as you keep me informed." Then Valfort pulled out a small pouch of gold. "I will even give you this." He dropped the binding spell, knowing his new acquaintance would not run. He was too greedy.

Holding out his grubby hands, the man eyed the pouch with delight. "Is it gold?" he asked excitedly.

Valfort snickered. "Of course... more than you've probably ever seen in your miserable life!" He tossed it to the man. "And there's more where that came from if you do what I ask!"

Quickly pulling the bag open, the man pulled out a coin and bit it just to be sure it was real. "Oh, I will find him, I promise. I haven't had a chance to work on something good like this since he found me."

"I can see that, my friend. You have quite obviously been down on your luck for some time." Valfort looked around the shack. "Is this where you stay?"

The man shook his head. "No. It has too many holes and lets light in. I dig a hole in the woods outside town to sleep. Safer than getting caught here. Only reason I'm still living."

Realizing he had the perfect way to secure the man's trust, Valfort sucked in a deep breath. "What if I told you I was willing to provide a steady, modest income for you, and a decent lair where you would be comfortable?"

Suspicion filling his eyes, the man took a step back. "Why would you do that?"

"Leaving the Mastric's tribe is next to impossible for a lower ranked individual. For me, it will mean overcoming serious challenges." Valfort paused and turned to gaze at him, all pretenses set aside. "You see, I am Mastric's eldest son... his firstborn. He is neither kind nor merciful in his treatment of any of his children, but with me, he takes special delight in being cruel because I am the first. I bear no love for him and even less for my fellow elders."

His host stared at him in surprise, shocked at who he was speaking to, and surprised by his candor. "That don't sound like something I would want either," he replied. "I suppose I been lucky because I don't know how to read. So nobody of note sought me out like that."

Valfort frowned, realizing he had been approaching this man all wrong. "I apologize. I did not even ask your name. So, let us start with that. What do they call you?"

"Hehe! They call me Rat, but me mum named me Justin." He looked sad for a minute. "She died long ago. I think she were the only person in the world who ever cared about me. Our masters don't expect us to live, so no names, no relationship, just work if you survive and none you get paid for." Glancing at the gold in his hand, he paused, looking thoughtful. "Hey... you get out of there, you'll be wanting a servant, no?"

Unfastening his cloak, Valfort handed it over. "As a matter of fact, I will. And I provide any servant of mine with decent clothing and lodging, as well as an education."

Justin grinned. "I could work for you. I'm good at finding things, I am. Master won't care if I work for someone else. As long as I do what job they give me, I am free to go anywhere I like and do what I please."

"Exactly what is your job?" Valfort asked, curious what job an eighth generation, so weak they were known only as beasts, could do that was important.

"Nice, this. Thanks." Justin put the cloak on and stroked its soft material with a smile. "Me job? I gather information on things they want to know. I can get into Alliance territories unseen and without danger of being discovered 'cause I don't have much of a birthright. No detectible power, get it? I report back what I find."

Valfort realized his new friend could be very valuable to him indeed. "That is a useful talent... one I may well have need of in future. Mastric watches me fairly close right now because he does not trust me. So having a friend on the outside could make it easier for me to get information in and out."

"Well, if you're giving them information what helps with the fight, my master will pass you up the chain to his boss when he sees your honest." Justin walked over and looked out the window. "Well, sun's not far from rising. I got to find some place to hole up for the night. It takes a bit to reach the outskirts."

Walking over and joining him, Valfort nodded. "True... or I could help you get a place tonight, so you no longer have to go to the outskirts." He held up his arm and sliced it open, and then offered it to Justin. "You said you wish to work for me, so, drink up. It's time for a new beginning..."

Do you want to know what happens to Reivn and his bloodline? Join thousands of fans and get your free content before it's gone forever! Don't miss this exclusive offer! https://www.krfraser.com/discoverdraegonstorm

## *About the Author –*

K.R. Fraser spent her childhood in Europe, visited multiple countries and experienced different cultures around the globe. She is fluent in three languages and knowledgeable in four more. She began theater and dance training at age three and was composing music by age eleven. She continued these studies into her young adult years.

Ms. Fraser developed an interest in books very young, and by fourteen had written her first collective of poetry, several of which were published worldwide in later years. At age sixteen, she began writing short stories and it became a life-long love. Her first short story in the horror genre, The Cycle, was published in 2006 and presently remains in circulation. She has since published several other works, has been seriously writing for more than twenty years and has worked as an editor for more than ten. She completed her first Associate's degree in multimedia in 2009, and then went on to achieve her Bachelor's and Master's in the media industry. Her works include award-winning poetry, short stories and news articles in various subjects of interest.

K.R. Fraser's work is ground-breaking and imaginative. Her use of imagery and character dialogue keeps you on the edge of your seat from beginning to end. This amazing series will easily carry your imagination to new heights and leave you begging for more.

*"Writing is a passion that will live in me until I close my eyes for the last time."*

*~ K.R. Fraser ~*

Lightning Source UK Ltd.
Milton Keynes UK
UKHW020759110821
388656UK00002B/285